Also by Sarah Moore Fitzgerald

Back to Blackbrick
The Apple Tart of Hope
A Very Good Chance
The List of Real Things
A Strange Kind of Brave
All the Money in the World

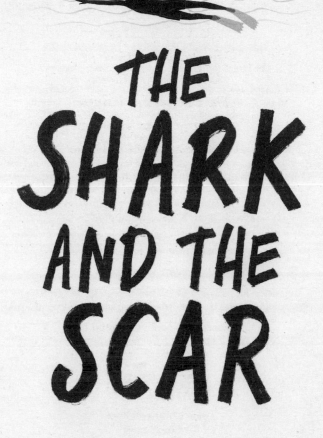

THE SHARK AND THE SCAR

SARAH MOORE FITZGERALD

Orion

ORION CHILDREN'S BOOKS

First published in Great Britain in 2022 by Hodder & Stoughton

1 3 5 7 9 10 8 6 4 2

A CIP catalogue record for this book
is available from the British Library.

ISBN 978 1 510 10416 7

Typeset in ITC Stone Serif Std by Jouve (UK), Milton Keynes
Printed and bound in Great Britain by Clays Ltd, Elcograf S.p.A.

The paper and board used in this book
are made from wood from responsible sources.

Orion Children's Books
An imprint of
Hachette Children's Group
Part of Hodder & Stoughton Limited
Carmelite House
50 Victoria Embankment
London EC4Y 0DZ

An Hachette UK Company
www.hachette.co.uk

www.hachettechildrens.co.uk

For Hughie

CHAPTER 1

JAY

W hen Jay Danagher finally woke up, he could only stare for a long time into the night-dimmed room. The whole right side of his body was stiff and swollen. Bandages covered his shoulder, his torso, his leg. It hurt to move. A cuff on his left bicep growled to life without warning, filling with air, then squeezing his arm tight before deflating again. All around him monitors bleeped and hissed.

In a cloud of half-consciousness he tried to remember what had happened, but the effort felt useless and exhausting – as if he was opening his eyes under mud-blackened water or grasping at the slippery handle of a thick, locked door.

At first he didn't see his father, who was sleeping in a chair right next to him, very close. But as his eyes adapted, the shape of his dad became clear.

'Dad?' he said in a gluey whisper. 'Where am I? What happened?'

Jay's dad jolted awake like someone who'd been stung by a wasp.

'You're in hospital, buddy,' he said, leaning forward, studying his son's face. 'You're OK. I've been right here the whole time.'

There were semi-circles of grey – like stains or bruises – under his dad's eyes.

And in the breath of that moment a collection of images came back to Jay, flung in confusing order on the beach of his disjointed memory.

The sparkle of the sea; a sudden frenzied chaos; a churning, a splashing; his body, caught up in an unwilling slow-motion dance; a reddening explosion of blood; a feeling of being pushed up above the surface, gasping for air; the raggy groan of his own voice; a horrible roar, like an engine or a lion; a scream somewhere, high-pitched and hysterical.

He could remember a sickening, dragging pain and how this had overtaken him and that he had not been able to withstand the pull of the dark. There had been a tiny instant of peace as his world had blurred and faded. And then after that: nothing.

Nothing, that is, until he'd woken to find himself here in a hospital bed with the bleeping machines and the high walls and the tired face of his father in this strange new season of blankness.

Drops of liquid fell in wet, clear beads from a tiny opening in a tube above him and inched along a milky pipe, making their way into his arm.

'Pain control, just for the moment,' his dad explained. 'Might make you feel a bit woozy.'

It was true. Jay's head felt full of fog and everything seemed blurred and distant; even his dad, who was right there.

'What happened?' Jay asked again.

'Don't you remember?'

'Why else would I be asking?' said Jay, whose first effort at smiling felt more like a wince.

'Let's not talk about any of it yet,' his dad said, all gentle and soft. 'We've got to focus on your recovery now. There'll be plenty of time for everything else once you're stronger. You're on the mend, buddy. That's the main thing. That's really all that matters.'

Sitting at the uninjured side, Dad took careful hold of Jay's left hand and kissed it, and kissed it, and kissed it again.

'Hey, knock it off,' said Jay, which is a thing he often said to his dad, and because of this, and for other reasons to do with love and connection and recognition and relief, the two of them began to laugh.

'That sounds more like my Jay,' said Dad, with a funny-sounding catch in his throat.

But Jay did not feel like himself. The laughing made forks of pain branch through his body like lightning. His brain was muddled. The words of his many questions could not form properly in his head or in his mouth. Even keeping his eyelids open felt like an awesome effort. He wanted to say a million more things, but he'd become suddenly aware that they weren't alone, and he was silenced by a new presence.

She was standing at a distance, her face smooth and smiling, her long nails varnished black. Had she been there the whole time? Silver bracelets clinked on her wrists as she clasped her hands together.

Jay stared at her, a shock of warmth flooding over him. 'Mum?' he said, instantly hating the way his voice had filled with impulsive, stupid hope.

'Oh no, no, no,' blurted his dad quickly, coughing a bogus cough.

As usual, when it came to anything to do with his mother, Jay's hope had been of the deluded variety, for this woman standing in front of him was not his estranged and long-absent mum, who as it turned out, had not rushed to be at his side in his moment of greatest need.

'This is Lonnie,' Dad said in English and then in French, dragging a sleeve across his eyes, 'Lonnie Lavelle.'

'*Sais-tu pourquoi tu es ici?*' Lonnie asked, and when Jay didn't answer she repeated the question in English – 'DO YOU KNOW WHY YOU ARE HERE?' – more loudly than she needed to.

Jay still did not know, but by then his curiosity, which had first been sharp and urgent, had somehow become blunted. He was glad when his dad interrupted.

'Listen, Lonnie, I'm going to discuss it with him by himself, just like you suggested. No need for anyone else to intervene. Say it to the others. *I*'ll be the one to tell him everything.'

Lonnie gave a nodding, knowing smile.

'Quite right, *bien sûr*, exactly as it should be,' she agreed. 'Now if you'll excuse me, I will alert the medical team that Jay is awake! Jay is lucid!'

'You don't have to know everything in one go,' Jay's dad whispered to him after she'd dashed away. 'You can take your time. Fill in the pieces bit by bit, in whatever order you like.'

Soon the doors were swinging open. A confusion of activity swirled around Jay and his father then – the clanging, rustling, steely loudness that happens when hospital people become urgently busy and full of purpose.

A tall doctor with a bald head and horn-rimmed glasses appeared first.

He spoke in English. 'My name is Dr Pierre Lambert, but you must call me Pierre.' Pierre put his hand on Jay's dad's shoulder and said, 'How are you doing, Patrick? Have you two had a chance to catch up?'

'We're going to do that gradually. Plenty of time,' his dad replied. 'I'll be talking to him about the accident, so you only need to fill him in on what's happened since he got here.'

Pierre nodded. 'Jay. Hello. You have been in an induced coma for almost four weeks,' he explained, pulling from his pocket a tiny torch that looked like a pen.

'Four what?' said Jay.

'Weeks,' repeated Pierre. 'You've had two operations to repair your injuries.' Pierre pointed to Jay's side and his neck. 'This upper part of the wound is mending nicely by itself. And now that you have come round, here begins your process of recovery! You and I will be taking charge of that together!' Pierre shone the torch into Jay's eyes.

'Hey, stop!' said Jay, squirming as much as he was able, and squinting from the glare.

'Ha, this is good!' said Pierre, turning to Jay's dad. 'Barely awake, and already he's giving orders. That's the spirit. Yes! An excellent sign!'

By then Jay was feeling too drowsy to care and closed his eyes, thinking he would fall asleep. Instead, he became suspended in a new space between waking and sleeping, where he couldn't talk or keep his eyes open, but could still hear the voices around him.

'It's going well, isn't it?' The edges of his father's voice sounded nervous. 'Especially since he's woken up. He's going to be OK now, right?'

Jay could feel the warmth and shift of what he thought must be the doctor, sitting gently at the very end of the bed.

'Patrick, listen –' Pierre spoke slowly to his father – 'I'm responsible for your son's recovery, and I am going to do everything I possibly can to make sure he's going to be OK.'

Jay's tiredness overtook him and he found himself slipping, as he often did in those early days, deep and fast, into another thick and troubled sleep.

He dreamed he was surfing and at first that felt good, except that in his dream when he looked down, the water was made of blood, and his right leg looked mangled and was covered in streaks of something slick and black, like oil.

When he woke, it was dark again. Jay was glad that his dad was beside him in the chair, but also glad to see that he was asleep. A bleakness had crept inside Jay's heart that he would not have been able to explain.

In the days that followed Pierre sometimes came into the ward wearing a clown nose, or giant glasses, or a silly hat. Jay would do his best to smile. 'Good one, Pierre,' he'd say, or 'Nice hat, man.'

But secretly he wished Pierre had the common sense to realise he wasn't a little kid and that it was going to take more than childish accessories to cheer him up.

Everyone became obsessed with what Jay should eat. He felt permanently queasy. His throat was scratchy and rough. Food was the last thing on his mind.

Lonnie was a recovery counsellor with a specialism in nutrition after trauma.

'We must begin immediately a programme of proper nutritional intake. It's essential for good healing,' she said.

Someone else appeared wearing a huge white apron. Her name was Marie-Bernard. She had butterfly clips in her hair and carried a tray on which there was a basket of bread, a packet of sugar, a dish of butter, a glass of milk, two bars of chocolate, a pot of yoghurt, a banana, a pear and a nectarine. Solemnly Marie-Bernard put this on the wheelie table, like she was presenting Jay with a very extravagant prize.

Every time he took a bite of anything, his dad seemed overjoyed, so even though eating felt like a chore, Jay knew he must try his best.

Maybe it was the pain relief, Jay thought, that made him feel too numb to enjoy the taste of food, or the sound of music, or the subject of thoughts, or memories of the past, or plans for the future.

Many more times he thought again to ask his dad what had happened, but that strange mix of listlessness and fear had clouded things between them. He was too frightened to look at his injuries and worried that the damage to his body might not be repaired. Conversations about any of this felt hard to start and unpredictable in their direction, and, besides, his dad had said it was too soon. There was no one in the world Jay trusted more, so he took his dad's advice, and listened to his own instincts and decided to avoid the subject. Whatever the accident was, it must have been horrible. He was happy not to have to know about it just yet.

Every day at three a nurse called Tom came to change Jay's bandages. This was the only time his dad left the room.

'Little scratch coming up,' Tom would warn, before plunging a needle into Jay's arm. A warm whoosh would seep through him, and an even stranger, even more distant feeling would come over him, and a fusion of jumbled thoughts would slide out of his brain and down, down, somewhere deep and unreachable.

When Tom changed the dressings Jay would turn his head to the wall, and squeeze his eyes shut and not speak until it was finished and Dad was back in the room. But Tom was a chatty sort of guy, and as the days went on, he managed to get Jay to talk a little – about his favourite sport (surfing obviously) and the best boards for a beginner since Tom was thinking of taking it up, and advice about what part of the coast would suit a learner.

As their time together turned from days to weeks, Tom and Jay slowly made their way towards the real subject.

10

'Hey, Jay,' he said one day. 'Your dad has asked me not to talk about the accident, so I won't. But if you ever want to ask me about your injury, just let me know, OK?'

Jay said no thanks.

But a couple of days later, Tom said, 'You know, you don't always have to close your eyes for this bit. Maybe if you saw it, it wouldn't feel so scary.'

'What's it like?' Jay found himself able to ask.

'Well, I wouldn't exactly call it beautiful. But it's getting a lot better,' Tom said, carefully unwrapping the wound. 'Why don't you have a quick look? You'll need a mirror for some of it. I can hold one up if you like.' Tom pulled a round mirror with a handle from his bandage bag to show Jay what he meant. It was this gentle advice and this practical suggestion that gave Jay the courage to face his injury for the first time.

In the mirror he could see that it started right up at his neck, just underneath his ear, carving a wide bloody, jagged stripe down the whole right side of his body, with metal stitches like gigantic staples.

But it wasn't the crooked bruised bits on his neck or on his chest or torso that shocked him. What had been most difficult to look at was where, at the top of his thigh, the injury darkened and deepened. It felt like his leg had been replaced with someone else's.

11

It was bloated and purple, twice its normal width, as if he'd been badly sewn together like some horror-movie monster.

'It won't always look like that,' said Tom, glancing at Jay's face, which had started to tremble. 'The swelling protects your body. Helps it mend. Are you OK?'

Jay said he was fine, just tired and in need of sleep. In those foggy days the distant, dreamy feelings often made it hard for him to tell the difference between what was real and what was the fake invention of his scrambled mind. A thousand times he longed to talk to his best friend, Louis, or to text his other friends from school or the gang from the surf club, but a thousand times the impulse would evaporate in a mist of drowsiness. Vaguely he wondered where his phone was. He hadn't seen it since he'd woken up.

'When am I going to get out of here?' he sighed when he woke again, and when Tom had gone and his dad was settled in the bedside chair. But his dad didn't reply, and Jay wondered whether or not he'd asked the question or just imagined having asked it and either way he felt too weak and flat to ask it again.

Personally he couldn't imagine himself ever being able to stand up straight, or walk, or run, or jump or do the things he once thought he'd always be able to do.

What began to haunt him most, now that he'd seen the state of his injury, was the fear – the darkest fear – that he would never surf again. That he'd never paddle like a madman out towards delicious mountains of foam. That he'd never watch a wave as it came tumbling towards him – gathering its power as he summoned his; that he'd never rise up on his board or flip or glide, high and strong, on one of those magic rolling curves. That he'd never dart like an arrow on the surface of the sea.

Jay lay back on the pillow. Tears pushed into his eyes and crept hotly down each side of his face.

Pierre was there suddenly, standing at his bed like a tower, and Jay's dad had drooped into the chair, sipping a small paper cup full of tea, dismayed at the sight of his son's tears.

'What is it, Jay? You must talk to us. Is there anything you would like to know?' Pierre asked.

'Will I ever be the same as I was before?' Jay blurted, each word feeling like a little knot.

'Jay,' said Pierre, and it looked like there might have been tears glistening behind those horn-rimmed glasses too. *'Ecoute moi. Regarde moi.'*

Jay waited, hoping the doctor was about to say something he could believe in.

'When you are badly injured, it feels as if nothing

will ever be the same. I understand this. These will be your darkest days. You must bring fortitude and energy. You are young and your body has the power to recover but you must summon your steel. It is OK to cry. You have suffered. But from now on this kind of sadness will only weaken you. Now comes the time for toughness. Are you tough, Jay?'

'I don't think so.'

'You are. Otherwise you wouldn't be here. Plus, you're an Irish boy, is this not true?'

'Well, my dad's Irish,' said Jay, 'so, yeah, I guess.'

'No guess about it! Irish people are warriors, *ne sont-ils pas*, Patrick?'

Jay's dad nodded his head meekly, sipping tea from the tiny cup, looking as un-warriorish as it's possible to look.

'It is the time to gather your Celtic spirit. It is the time to call on the same strength you've needed to get this far,' said Pierre, looking sternly at Jay. 'Do you think you can try that for me?'

Jay nodded his head and closed his eyes and felt thankful that Pierre was working so hard for him, but guilty that he had not yet been able to find the hope he was going to need.

Not long after this, Lonnie began to ask strange, difficult-to-answer questions.

14

'If your emotions were a colour, what colour do you think they would be?'

Jay shrugged. It was hard to explain. Nothing had a colour really. He didn't feel happy and he didn't feel sad. He didn't feel hope and he didn't feel despair. He was tempted to say 'blizzard-white' or 'foggy grey' but somehow he didn't think those were the answers Lonnie was looking for. Instead, he said, 'Maybe red? Dark red?' And Lonnie said this was excellent, and Jay felt as if he'd passed some sort of test.

'Do you have any questions you'd like to ask? Is there anything you'd like to discuss?' But whenever she said this, Jay's dad would lean in closer and speak loudly and say, 'It's OK, Lonnie, if Jay has any more questions, he's going to ask me. Isn't that right, Jay?'

Jay felt a weird loneliness. He longed for the days when he wasn't surrounded by a medical team. He missed his friends. He missed the apartment and the sound of the waves when he slept. He missed his surfboard and his chats with Louis. He even missed school.

But Pierre had been right. There were better days ahead. The day, when changing his bandages, Tom said, 'Look, Jay, I think you should look at this again,' and when he did, he saw that the scar, while still red and still huge, wasn't quite as horrible any more. The day they took away the drip with the strong drugs, and Jay found that he could bear a pain that no longer felt so deep or sharp. The day he got out of bed and stood. The day he went to the exercise room and began to test his growing strength. He was summoning some steel, like Pierre had said, and even though a big part of him still felt bleak and scared, there was a glimmer of brightness now. At least that's what everyone told him.

'Dad, I think I'm ready,' he said one evening over Marie-Bernard's scones, back from an afternoon of rehab with Jacques and Beatrice, the physiotherapists.

'Ready for what?'

'To ask you about the accident.'

'Great,' said his dad, straightening up and brushing crumbs off his lap. 'Shoot. Anything you like. Whatever you want to know.'

'What happened? What happened to me?'

His father grew still and silent, and pulled at his Velcro watchstrap. *Scritch. Scritch. Scritch.*

'Are you sure you're ready to hear?'

'The way I see it,' said Jay, who'd given it a lot of thought. 'If I'm going to recover properly, I need to know what I'm recovering *from*.'

His dad looked over one shoulder and then the other, and gently put his hand on Jay's good arm. 'Do you still not remember any of it?'

'Not much.'

'OK, then why don't we start with you telling me what you do remember?'

Jay concentrated. 'We were down at Dellabelle Cove the day before my birthday, just as we'd planned.'

'Yes, correct,' said his dad.

'And I was in the water with my snorkel and my goggles and my new earphones.'

'Yes, you were. Exactly right.'

'And then . . .'

The room wobbled slightly in front of Jay. He was reaching again beyond the frail shreds of memory, grabbing at disjointed scraps.

'There was something big in the sea, and massive pain and blood and you shouting and someone else's voice screaming, and a roaring sound, like an engine . . . and . . . well . . . that's it. That's pretty much everything I've got.'

'You must have blacked out.'

17

'Yeah, so, Dad, listen, I've been trying to figure it out myself, and I think I know what it was,' said Jay.

His dad stood up, turned away from his son, and lifted a sign that was dangling on the door handle. PATIENT RESTING. DO NOT DISTURB.

He opened the door, hung the sign on the outside, pushed the door carefully closed again with the flats of both his hands, sat back down and leaned in very close. He took a deep, slow, heavy breath and patted the bedclothes as if to smooth them out, even though they were already smooth.

'OK, so what do you think?' asked his dad. 'What do you think happened?'

'I reckon I was attacked.'

'By what?'

'By a shark.'

There was a flicker on Jay's dad's face and a widening in his eyes, and he exhaled – relieved, Jay supposed, that the truth had finally been spoken.

'That's exactly it!' his dad said. 'How did you guess?'

CHAPTER 2

JESS

When I was very small, I fell into the sea off Gillanane Rock. It was only for, like, half a second. I was in a buggy and the brakes were accidentally left off, and it was a windy day and the buggy blew over the grassy head and down into the wild Atlantic. It wasn't a huge drop, and obviously I didn't drown. I was grand a few seconds after it happened, and I've been grand ever since. I've no idea why everyone keeps going on about it. It wasn't a proper emergency or anything. There were loads of people there and I was easy to save.

Babies are born with the ability to swim. Everyone says I couldn't possibly remember, but I do. I wasn't scared. I *liked* it – the split-second glimpse of that different magical world. When I opened my eyes under the water, it felt as if music began to play, and there were shapes and colours I had never seen and feelings I had never felt: feelings of excitement and possibility and adventure and freedom.

From then on I was obsessed. I spent the rest of my childhood dreaming about swimming and diving and surfing and snorkelling. Any chance I got, I'd plunge underwater to feel again that magic change from the dry world up here to the wet, juicy, gurgling, fizzing world down there.

The mishap on the headland became the curse of my life. Not because it happened, but because of how everyone acted after it. On that day both my parents and my two siblings jumped in after me. It wasn't even that deep. The only reason I cried was because Esme hugged me so fiercely it hurt, and because my dad was crying, which is the kind of thing that's bound to alarm a baby.

It was no big deal. It was a very small, tiny deal, in fact. If my family was the slightest bit normal, no one would even talk about it any more. But they're not normal. They're practically famous for obsessing over trivial things. It's impossible to explain how annoying this is. Every single time I wanted to go for a paddle or a dip there always had to be this huge diplomatic negotiation in our house with family members sitting round the kitchen table discussing the details and instructions as if I was a project.

'You paddle with her, Charlie; the rest of us will stand guard on the beach,' Esme would say.

'I'll bring the loudhailer in case of emergency,' Dad would chip in. That kind of thing. It was enough to make me want to run screaming from my house and never come back.

They made me get hundreds of lessons in the Cloncannor Hotel pool that no one swims in on account of there being the proper sea right across the road. And the four of them came to every one of those lessons and sat watching from the benches like lifeguards, alert to the possibility of me being pulled under at any moment by some invisible force.

For years and years I was only allowed in the pathetic shallows, and as a result of this all my water-related skills were woefully underdeveloped. At that rate there was no way I was going to catch up with Esme or Charlie, who didn't just teach advanced surfing classes in the big waves in summer but surfed through the winter – a thing I would never be allowed to do, or to think about – and they won competitions in places like Donegal and Sligo and they'd been to Australia and America. The reason our surf school was famous was because of them.

Most of my life consisted of sitting on the beach watching and wishing I was them, and cursing the windy day long ago, and cursing my family for being so bizarre and unreasonable, and cursing the eight-year gap between me and them, which was like a wide river that I could not cross. I was always going to be the youngest and there'd always be this massive distance between us and they were going to spend the rest of their lives underestimating what I was capable of.

So, needless to say, when they sat at the table announcing a new promise to me, I was amazed. At first I literally couldn't believe what they were saying. After years of begging, this spring, this *May*, I was going to be allowed to surf out in the bay on the big waves.

They told me this at Christmastime. Mistake number one. Like a prisoner scratching tally marks on their cell wall, I'd been counting the days on the calendar since then.

Dad said the whole point of time is that it passes. And it would pass much more quickly if I stopped fixating on it. But time seemed to be breaking its own rules – moving slower than misery. I was sure I'd have grown old by the end of April, like some fairy-tale girl, or be dead, or for some other time-mangled reason I'd be past caring. But when the day finally did come, I cared more than I ever had. As a matter of fact, I was ecstatic.

I shouldn't have been. I mean, I should have known there'd be some disaster or other. But it's staggering the way hope and joy can smother the ability for rational thought.

Mam told me to cool my jets. According to her, it was vitally important not to get hyped up or overexcited.

'Listen, missy-moo,' is what she said. 'I hope you realise it's not a matter of dashing off into the deep. You've got to remember everything we've said. Just because the season's here, you're not to go around thinking that you'll instantly be let out there. There's still a huge amount of preparation and training to get through. Look at me, Jessie. Hello, Jess? Jessie! Jessica! Are you even listening?'

I do accept that the instructions had been made very clear, not just by Mam but by Dad and Charlie and then over and over again for ever by Esme until I was sick of her.

Apparently I was going to need at least a couple of weeks of practice in the shallows to 'reacquaint' myself with the water after the long winter, and then I'd need more time again to work on my technique, which involved putting the board on the sand and *pretending* I was surfing, which, for everyone's information, is minus-zero fun.

I knew it was wrong. Technically, I was still in the pre-permission phase when I swam out to the breakers with my own surfboard. My parents had got the board for me months ago, and for that whole time it had been standing against the shed like a patient friend, glimmering and perfect, white with a zigzag stripe of blue lightning. And, OK, I know I wasn't supposed to go by myself. And I know I'd been told approximately a thousand times. But it wasn't as if I was being deliberately rebellious or anything. It's just that those terms and conditions – well, they simply flew right out of my head. There's no other way to explain it.

None of them believed I just forgot, but that's what happened.

'THIS IS THE YEAR!' was what my brain kept shouting, and 'THIS IS THE SEASON' and 'THERE ARE THE WAVES.'

Those facts were loud and seductive, like sirens. Strictly speaking, I wasn't really on my own in the water. Esme was out there already with her class of advanced weekend surfers. And I suppose you could say I paddled out alone, but even that's a bit picky if you ask me, on account of Esme being out in the water and on account of me being very safe with my life jacket clipped tightly on and my ankle firmly attached to the leg rope of my brand-new board.

As soon as Esme saw me, she lost the plot. According to her, I'd committed an actual crime. She'd grabbed on to me very roughly and shouted, 'Excuse me, class! Hello, everyone, I'm afraid we're going to have to finish early because of Jess here. Everyone! Please follow me back to shore! I do apologise!'

And then, silent and fuming, she'd pulled me towards the beach and out of the water like I was a disgusting piece of rubbish that needed to be removed from the ocean and thrown away.

I tried to explain, but there was no point. The sea had been gorgeous, I said, and the surf was perfect, and I was afraid the waves might never be as good as they looked right at that moment and, besides, I'd been waiting so long.

Esme wasn't having any of it. After hauling me back to the shallows, she grabbed me by the wrist in this horrible, forceful way, and she told me I was a very bad person who could never again be trusted.

Charlie was on the beach and he witnessed it all. He didn't come to my defence, even though Esme

25

was basically assaulting me. I kept my dignity by refusing to look her in the eye, staring instead at the wetsuits, which were draped over the iron railings like deflated seals. Charlie was busy hammering the signs – FLANAGANS' SURF SCHOOL: LESSONS THIS WAY – into the grassy bank at the edge of the sand and sticking up red cardboard arrows pointing towards where Esme had marched me out of the shallows, back to the dry.

The whole time Esme was doing her fury walk up the beach, holding on to me, and I was trying to get away from her. But Esme's grip is like a vice and I could not escape and so had no option but to trot along beside her while she whispered words of seething accusation. 'You've blown it now. This is the complete last straw! After all your promising and agreeing in front of Mam and Dad. After all the begging.'

'What? What, Esme? What have I even done?'

'What do you think?'

'I think nothing! Mam was finished with the baby lessons in the shallows and I've been helping her the whole morning and she *told* me I didn't have to come home with her. Mam made it *completely clear* I was allowed to stay to wait for you, but, Esme, I waited for ages, like I was told, and you kept on not coming in. I thought you were literally *never* going to. You were already *there* and the waves were so good. I was acting on logic,' I argued. 'That's what I was doing! Seizing the day! Grabbing the chance!'

'Just stop, Jess, please. Stop twisting things round like you always do. In a way I blame myself because, honestly, I should have known. Go straight home. You're not to even think about getting back into that water.'

'Yeah, well, you can't order me around. I mean, do you own the ocean? No, you don't. It's a free world.'

'Jessie, I swear, if you don't shut up—'

'What? What will you do?'

'Never mind. Go home.'

'But this is so mean.'

'I don't care. Jess, you're impossible.'

'Once you're born you've basically proved you're possible,' I shouted back at her. 'So that's a stupid thing to say.'

Charlie was jogging towards us now, still with the wooden mallet in his hand, and a big curious face. 'What's going on?'

'I literally can't put up with this any more,' said Esme, fury purpling her cheeks. 'She's banned. That's it. Banned from the sea for the rest of the year.'

It would have been nice for him to come to my defence, but Charlie knows better than to argue with Esme when she's having a meltdown.

'Do me a favour, will you? Make sure she goes home. Get her out of my sight.'

I turned to him. 'Charlie, save me from her, protect me, stand up for me,' I pleaded. But Charlie is Esme's twin, and the two of them have this secret code of loyalty, and I remembered that as I watched him with his hands on his hips. He stared up at the sky in a way that looked as if he too was praying for patience. I was never going to be allowed in the water again.

CHAPTER 3

JAY

'You can't tell anyone else,' said his dad.

'About what?'

'About the shark.'

'Why not?"

'Because it's a secret. It's against the law to discuss it. I've signed a non-disclosure agreement about the whole thing, and we must never speak about it or we'll ruin tourism around Dellabelle Cove for ever.'

'What?'

'Look, the point is, it can't go outside this room. It has to stay between the two of us. Right?'

But something was happening to Jay as the fact of the shark attack reverberated inside him like ripples in a pool. This was the moment when he stopped feeling small and weak and broken. He sat up straight and strong. His numbness and fear made way for something else – something that was vivid and clear. It felt like courage. It looked like pride.

'What kind of shark was it?'

Jay's dad paused and closed his eyes for a second as if he couldn't bear the memory of it.

'A great white.'

'Whoa! What the heck?'

'I know, unbelievable, huh?'

Jay looked down at his body with a new sense of respect. 'I guess that makes me lucky to be alive. How did I escape?'

'Oh, gosh, well, you know, it happened very fast and I couldn't see clearly, but, Jay, you must have fought like hell. You must have kicked like a trooper, braver than an army. Whatever you did, you scared him off, because that shark spat you right back up on to the beach. Picked the wrong boy to mess with, that's for sure.'

Jay laughed. It still hurt a bit but he didn't mind, especially because his dad laughed again too. There was a new sunshine in the room. The weird shocked, swollen feelings were beginning to fade.

There was something great about being a shark bite survivor. He was on the verge of saying this to his dad but by then another important question needed to be asked. A question that had been tumbling around inside him for a long time.

'Where is she, Dad? Did she come? Did she see me?'

His dad gripped the steel tube of Jay's bed. 'Who? Did who come?'

'Mum, of course. Who do you think?'

And suddenly, more than anything, Jay hoped his mother had shown up like she'd promised at last, that she'd seen him in the water at Dellabelle Cove fighting off a great white shark – for the most dramatic family reunion in the whole of history.

His dad grabbed the bed even tighter, his knuckles like small white blades. He stared at the blank wall behind Jay's head.

'No,' he whispered.

'She never came?'

'Exactly that. That's it. Never came.'

'Have you talked to her? Does she know we're here?'

His dad sighed. 'Jay, listen, what can I say? You know your mother.'

Jay did not know his mother. That was the whole point – and it was the reason they'd gone to Dellabelle Cove in the first place. They were supposed to meet her there. It was going to be the first time he'd seen her since he was a baby.

'Look, I don't want to speak badly of her, but the truth is your mother's not reliable. No one has been able to count on her. She likes to make a big dramatic entrance every so often, but then she disappears for years on end.

His dad was explaining this in a low voice now. Jay had to concentrate quite carefully to hear.

'I was worried about that whole arrangement from the start. I always thought it was a bad idea. Afraid she'd let you down. And that's what she did, Jay, in a spectacular manner.'

'There's nothing spectacular about not showing up, Dad.'

'No, sorry. Of course you're right. I knew how much you'd been looking forward to it and that you were relying on her to do what she promised. And then this terrible thing happened to you.'

'Yeah, well, nobody could have predicted this,' said Jay. 'You can't blame her for it.'

'No, I suppose not,' said his dad, looking down at his fingers.

By then Jay had a ton more questions, but it didn't seem to be the time to ask because his dad was tidying – clearing the teacups that Marie-Bernard hadn't been back for. 'This place is full of rubbish,' he said, peering into the bedside locker.

'Maybe Mum was just late? Did you try to call her?'

'It wasn't that . . . I don't think there's any way to get hold of her now. You know how difficult it's always been to contact her.'

Jay did know this. He'd only ever spoken to her on the phone four times in his life. The sound of her voice was vague and fuzzy. Plus, she had zero social media presence. He had one photograph of her but she was looking away, so he didn't know much more than the back of her head, which could have belonged to anyone with long light-brown wavy hair.

Jay's dad was pulling wrappers, empty bottles, used tissues and stale rice cakes from the locker and flinging them with high energy into the tall bin by the sink.

'But she must have heard about what happened. Weren't we on the news or in the papers?'

Something flashed across his dad's face then – a kind of darkening – as if a flock of tiny bats had swooped between them.

'Remember what I said. This is top secret. It wasn't on the news. It wasn't in the papers or on the TV.'

Jay frowned. 'What do the doctors think happened

then? What does Lonnie think? Don't they know about it?'

'Of course *they* know. But they can't discuss it, either. You mustn't talk to any of them. Right?'

'OK, calm down, Dad,' Jay said, who in spite of the rise in his energy levels felt tired again and could only see his father now through the tangled lashes of his own drooping eyelids. He did not want to go to sleep. He'd been asleep for far too long already, and important things were coming back to him.

'My earphones!' he said, remembering more. 'My brand-new earphones! And my phone! Did anyone find them?'

'No, they're gone,' his dad said, sitting down again and leaning forward, his head in his hands. 'To be honest, Jay, I don't want to think about any of it.'

'But maybe we can get them back? We could easily ask Louis or one of the guys from the club to go up to Dellabelle and see if there's any sign? The earphones are totally shockproof, impervious to water damage. And my phone was wrapped up in the orange towel. I left it at the bottom of the wooden steps – I remember now – safely away from the water. They could still be working perfectly. Those earphones are the best things I've ever owned. And, Dad, I haven't been able to text or talk to anyone. I need my phone. It's a basic human right.'

'What do you need it for in here? I'm always beside you.'

'I hate to break it to you but you're not the only person in my life. I'm going to need to text Louis. He's going to want to come to see me. It's been weeks. It's bad enough I'm here, but being cut off from everyone on top of it – that's a nightmare. We need to do something about it before I go totally mad.'

'Let me think about it.'

'There's nothing to think about.'

'Stop it, Jay. Just stop.'

His dad's voice was startlingly loud with a bitter sharpness to it that Jay did not recognise. He gazed at him in baffled silence.

Jay's dad slumped a little in the chair. 'I'm sorry, mate. I didn't mean to snap at you. The thought of those earphones torments me. If you hadn't had them on, you'd have heard the danger. You'd have had time to get out of harm's way. I can't forgive myself. What a stupid bloody gift. It's going to haunt me, Jay.'

Jay thought for a moment that his dad was going to cry, and he would have done anything to stop that from happening and so he began to scold himself. Of course Dad didn't want to talk about it any more – not the shark, not the earphones, not his mobile. It must have been a terrible thing to witness. It must be awful to be reminded of it.

Jay's dad looked towards the window at some distant painful place. A shadow hovered around his eyes, and he rubbed his face and sniffed, and Jay decided he'd wait a while before mentioning the phone again.

It turns out that once he started it, Jay's rehab was a full-time job. By the time he got back to his room after exercise and the physio, he was always wrecked. He wanted desperately to get back to normal, but in some ways the hospital had become his new normality, a cocoon, a bubble, away from the other parts of his life, and the doctors and nurses and Lonnie and Tom and Pierre and Marie-Bernard became like a new family.

Lonnie and his dad had become especially good friends. Sometimes they chatted for so long that Jay would feel the old exhaustion again and close his eyes, as if he was asleep. That way he could keep on listening but did not feel the pressure to speak. It was during one of those pretend sleeps that Jay heard her say, 'I love your accent, *Patrique*,' and then his dad laughed, making this flirty fake sighing noise at the end that Jay had definitely never heard before. His dad went on to tell Lonnie loads of things about himself that he barely told anyone, including that he was from Ireland, that he was an artist, that he would have had his first proper exhibition in Marseilles, only for Jay's injury.

He told her he had pictures of some of his paintings on his phone. Lonnie asked if she could see them, and then said they were magnificent.

'How did you end up here in France?' Lonnie asked in a whisper, thinking Jay was asleep when actually he was still mock-sleeping.

'Oh, well, that's its own story, I suppose.' Jay's dad chuckled. 'There wasn't much to stay in Ireland for in those days. My folks had a farm and after they died I just made the decision to sell up, make a new start. I was young then, and I'd only ever seen the south of France in the movies. Thought it was time for me to check it out for real. So when I arrived, between one thing and another, I met a woman, Elouisa. Elouisa Fougère. And then we had Jay, and not long after that she left us, and that's pretty much it.'

37

'Wow,' sighed Lonnie.

'It's just been me and him ever since. France became my permanent home, because, well, you know, his mother was gone, and he was still only a baby. He needed continuity in his life.'

'You're a wonderful father,' crooned Lonnie.

'Oh, I don't know about that.'

'Does he ever ask about Ireland?'

'All the time. He's obsessed with Denise Chaila, and of course he's heard about the surf on the west coast. The Wild Atlantic Way, they call it.'

'Sounds magnificent.'

'Yeah. He's always pestering me about a holiday or a visit. I love the memory of the place, but my folks are gone. Farm is sold. Haven't been back in twenty years.'

There was the sound of rustling as Jay continued to listen, and he kept on pretending to be asleep because opening his eyes would have felt like an invasion of some private moment that did not belong to him.

'And how are *you* these days, *Patrique*?'

Jay could sense the bedcovers moving a bit, as if his dad had grabbed on to them, maybe bunching them up in his hands.

'Oh, gosh, well, you know.'

Little airy puffs of laughter came from Lonnie. 'No, as a matter of fact, I don't. It's why I'm asking.'

A faltering chain of answers came falling out of his father. 'I'm relieved, and glad he's done so well,' he said. 'But I'm still angry, I'm still shocked about what happened. And, Jesus, the guilt, you know? That's what's tormenting me now. It was partly because of the earphones, you see.'

'Oh, but you must not blame yourself –' and again Lonnie sang Jay's dad's name in the French way – '*Patrique*. Have you two talked about what happened?'

'Yes, we have.'

'And how did that go?'

'What do you mean?'

'Well, it must have been a difficult conversation.'

Lonnie continued to talk – about how close Jay had been to death and how lucky it was he did not die, and what a miracle he was on the mend, and a blessing he hadn't lost his leg as Dr Lambert had at first feared he might.

'You need to take good care of yourself too, *Patrique*,' she began to advise. 'You mustn't forget what a shock you have endured and how it will take time to recover your sense of safety, your feelings of normality.'

'I'm fine,' said his dad, sniffing. 'I have to focus on Jay now. He's my only priority.'

Jay could hear her soft footsteps walking over to his dad's side of the bed and a new silence that went on for ages.

When Jay opened his eyes, Lonnie and his dad were standing very close together and they both jumped apart like they'd been electrified or something, and looked at Jay and burst out laughing in a way that made Jay wonder what was going on between the two of them. But he didn't ask. And they didn't say.

CHAPTER 4

JESS

'Come on, kiddo, no point in arguing. Let's go. You can explain on the way.' Maybe Charlie couldn't do anything to change Esme's mind, but at least he would listen, and I knew he'd understand.

'Talk about an overreaction. She says I've no patience. But, Charlie, when you've been longing for proper surf your whole life like I have, the shallows are an insult. Why does she get to do this to me?' I wailed.

'Because she's your big sister. It's her prerogative to boss you around – one of life's most basic laws.' Charlie was treating me like a baby too; it was obvious they were collaborating.

'You're making that up. If anything, she's breaking the law, actually, by violating my human rights.

41

I only did what anyone else would have done in the same situation.'

'Jessie, please.'

'I mean, anyone serious about becoming a surfer. Those waves don't come along every day, and who knows how long it might be before they come back again, and anyway, I can't stand having to listen to her, the boasting she does: "When I was in Hawaii" this, and "When I was in Rossnowlagh" that, and "I've conquered the waves on Bondi Beach." Charlie, she's such a pain.'

'OK, but think about it from her perspective. It's dangerous to do what you did. She probably had a heart attack when she saw you out there. Anyone would have.'

'I kept my board tie on. I never took this life jacket off. At first I didn't hear her shouting at me to go back. As a matter of fact, I thought she was giving me a beckoning wave.'

'You did not.'

'She thinks she's such a great teacher. But teachers are supposed to give you courage, not hold you back. She pulled me to shore herself, the whole way. In front of everyone.'

Charlie and I climbed the steps from the beach and walked through the dunes. He waved at the golfers on the seventh tee across the road, and they waved back.

'I can't tell you how mortifying it was. And now she's cancelled me. No breakers this year. That's what she said.'

'She'll calm down. Maybe she'll change her mind.'

'Don't be ridiculous. This is Esme we're talking about. When have you known her to change her mind about anything? What am I even going to do now? I've nothing planned for the rest of the spring or the whole of the summer. It's ruined, just because she decided to have a knicker-fit with me. I actually hate her.'

'You don't.'

'I can't think of anything worse.'

'I can,' said Charlie, his cheerful face turning serious. 'I can think of something much worse. What if you drowned out there?'

Since I was born, it was obvious the whole system of ordinary justice in my family had broken down. When they were years younger than me, Esme and Charlie spent their whole lives practically living beyond those breakers. But for me, there was a different set of rules. All because of that stupid time I fell into the sea.

*

'What are we going to do with you?' Mam moaned like I was a human disaster. I'd tried my best to explain how Esme had overreacted and that if Mam would just listen to me she'd be able to appreciate my side of the story.

In the end, to be fair, Charlie had tried. He said Esme had probably gone a bit over the top and that maybe it wasn't a hundred per cent fair to ban me from the sea. But Mam said that if I couldn't be trusted to obey the safety rules of the family, then she for one was a hundred per cent behind Esme.

'Oh, great!' I shouted. 'This is bleedin' great.'

Charlie began to laugh and Mam was like, 'What's funny?' and 'Where did Jess pick up such language?' and she whacked a tea towel in Charlie's direction as if she was sure he was to blame. And Charlie kept making faces to try cheering me up but it didn't do any good on account of there being a huge sunless cave of despair inside me.

Before he'd even taken off his boots in the hall, Mam was giving Dad an update.

If we talked about it any more I was pretty sure I'd actually vomit, so instead I sat looking out of the window and refusing to answer any more questions on the grounds that anything I said only made things worse.

In family arguments Dad was usually my last chance of having someone on my side. But when Esme and Mam joined forces, having someone on my side didn't make a difference. Once the two of them formed an alliance, I was basically screwed.

'It's because they love you,' Dad tried to explain. 'And they want you to be safe.'

'Right, Dad, that's a great help, thanks,' I said, but there was no point because he never gets sarcasm. When I told him my summer was ruined, he told me I was being 'defeatist'. He was right. I was defeated.

'Esme says she's never going to let me out there.'

'Never?'

'That's what she said, and you know her – the stubbornest person on the planet. So what will I do?'

'Well, if Esme won't have you at lessons, then you'd need to find a strong, responsible surfer who will. Someone who understands the sea and knows how to respect the water, and who can keep an eye on you at all times. Someone like Charlie.'

'Oh, brilliant, Dad, yeah. Charlie's going to Spain on Friday.'

'Is it this Friday?' said Dad, checking his watch. 'That came round fast.'

I was going to be abandoned to a sea-less solitude in my catastrophe of a life.

I went to my room and flung myself on the floor, cursing my paranoid parents, cursing my overbearing siblings, wishing that nobody loved me.

From my bedroom I have one of the best views of Cloncannor Beach. Its two curves and the line of the sea make it look a giant 'B'. In the middle of the B is Table Rock, big and grey and flat and great for sitting on – a well-known stone-skimming spot. Spring is always the best: the sun catches on the granite, which throws out random jets of silver light; the terns soar high above and dive like darts down into the deep and up again, leaving small sudsy scars on the surface of the water; the gulls gather, flapping and shrieking. Spring promises warmth and sunshine, but the winter wildness is still hanging around, and beyond the shallows the surf is rowdy and high and it sounds like it's whispering, beckoning. But all this was dull and joyless to me now.

I could hear Dad's footsteps creaking on the attic stairs. He knocked on the door.

'Stop, Dad, there's no point,' I said, but he came in anyway and sat at the end of my bed.

'We're not that bad, are we?'

'You're worse than bad, the lot of you. You're terrible.'

'What about ice cream in town? I saw Aidan Bannon's truck there, shined up and opened for the season.'

'I thought I was grounded.'

'Only from the water. Not from life. Not from ice cream.'

Aidan Bannon's ice creams were famous. Soft, rich, swirly vanilla, covered in rivulets of lime or strawberry sauce with a Flake plunged at an angle into the white creaminess. I sat up and sniffed. 'You know, Dad, ice cream might actually be a good idea. At least it'll get me out of this oppressive house for a while.'

'Precisely,' he said, handing me five euros.

'I'm sorry, Dad. I shouldn't have been so mean to you. You're actually the best.'

'It's only because you gave your sister such a fright. It'll blow over. Try not to be angry with them, Jessie.'

I didn't believe him, but still I said OK.

The reason Davy Flanagan is the best of company is because he's a dog. You don't have to explain anything to him and he doesn't bombard you with opinions or theories or unwanted advice.

Ice cream used to be the solution to every problem, and this was my first of the season. I hoped if I ate it slowly, then it would work its old magic, but it turned out to be nothing more than a temporary distraction. It didn't make anything better. For one thing I'd met Aidan in the town the other day, and he'd gone on about how he hadn't seen me in such a long time and said wasn't it just as well it was ice-cream season again or he might never see me at all. He didn't know that the reason for this was that me and his sons Cian and Jimmy weren't friends any more.

I still hated my sister, and I pretty much hated my brother and my mother. And for the rest of the summer the only person I would be able to rely on was Davy, and he wasn't even a person. I mean, he's the best dog in the world and everything, but sometimes you need human friends who you can talk to, and I didn't have any of those any more. And so that's pretty much how the summer that was supposed to be the best of my life became wrecked and ruined before it had even begun.

CHAPTER 5

JAY

As Jay's scar healed, it began to itch. Pierre said this was another excellent sign, but that it was vital not to scratch it. If Jay thought for a second that he might, he was to press the red button and a nurse would come with cream and oil.

Jay's mind was straightening up a bit, but his thoughts were not yet solid or clear, and there wasn't much he could do about the weird images that still sometimes appeared inside his head, weaving, snagging and bumping up against each other in a chaotic tangle, like the flapping and thrashing of peculiar dark-finned fish.

He was the only person he knew who'd ever been attacked by a shark. Like the itching of his scar, a spiky kind of curiosity began to vex him.

It was a gruesome thing to have happened, but it

was an interesting gruesome thing. How great would it be to be able to remember his fight for survival, to recall in clear detail how he had managed to confront and survive the attack of an actual shark?

One morning, after his dressings had been changed and his sheets were fresh and his dad seemed in a good mood, humming away, Jay thought he'd try raising the subject again.

'Dad?

'What?'

'Don't you think it's a great story?'

'What?'

'You know, the story of the shark, and what happened. Wouldn't it be good if I could tell other people about it?'

The angry bat-wing shadow darkened his father's face again.

'No, I do not think it would be a good story to tell anyone, ever. It's a very grave story. Remember what I said? Have you forgotten already?' Jay's dad swiped his hand through his hair and then spoke in a way that made Jay feel kind of sick.

'I don't expect to have to say this again, Jay. This

50

is top-secret stuff, not to be discussed with anyone. Right? I thought I'd made it clear to you. Did I not explain about the confidentiality agreement?'

'Yeah, you did but . . . It's just that—'

The echo of approaching footsteps from the corridor startled them both.

'So, one more time, Jay, I need to hear you promise, no more discussion about it, OK?'

'OK, fine, Dad, I promise.'

'That's a good lad.'

Lonnie was the owner of the footsteps. Now she was at the door carrying a tray. 'Does anyone in here fancy an afternoon pick-me-up?' she said, bright-eyed and kind-hearted, holding up two Frappucinos for her and his dad, and a melon cooler for Jay, like trophies.

'Do we what?' Jay's dad smiled as Lonnie swooshed in.

Jay felt bad about his dad's art exhibition. His dad had been putting the finishing flourishes to the last painting when they'd gone to Dellabelle, and the show was supposed to have been the following week. He could hardly bear to ask him about it, and, when he did, his dad said, 'Ah, sure, listen, buddy, you're not to worry about anything like that. None of that matters now,' which made Jay feel even worse. He was proud of his dad's brilliant work. There'd been ads in the paper and his paintings were full of wild and luminous colour. He had been just about to get famous for the beauty he could put on a canvas. Jay had wrecked that too.

His dad seemed to have put everything on hold. There were no spatters of paint on his tanned hands any more. These days it was as if he had only one job, which was to sit on the chair beside Jay's bed and never leave except to make some quick phone call or other, or talk to Lonnie or to go to the toilet.

It was a fluke that Lonnie arrived once to find Jay alone. She reached over and took his hand and held it for an embarrassingly long time. 'So your dad told you what happened, huh?'

Jay nodded.

'Good. Don't worry, I'm not going to ask you to talk about it, of course, but I want you to know that you're a very brave boy.'

'Thank you,' said Jay.

'And the important thing now is forgiveness. Don't hold on to any resentment. Don't nurture any blame.'

'I don't,' said Jay truthfully, because if anything, he was grateful to the shark for sparing his life.

Next time Lonnie came, she brought Frappucinos again with huge swirls of cream on top, and she pulled a chair up beside Jay's dad and put her hand flat on the fresh white sheet with her fingers splayed out like a starfish.

The morning's rehab had been especially energetic, and Jay actually did sleep for part of that afternoon. When he woke up he laughed at the sight of his dad.

'What happened to your hair?'

His dad shrugged.

'It's so messy and tufty. And your T-shirt!'

'What about it?'

'It's inside-out.'

Lonnie and his dad hadn't touched their Frappucinos, whose swirls of cream had collapsed into the cold coffee, by then more like a soggy-looking soup. When she came to clean the room, Marie-Bernard tut-tutted about the waste.

Another time, Jay woke to find Lonnie and his dad working on a crossword together. 'Simultaneous!' Lonnie announced delightedly, and Jay could see how pleased his dad was to have something else to do, even if it was just writing letters into little numbered boxes.

At first the exercise room had glowed with sparkling promise – parallel bars and weight machines and treadmills. By now he was making his way there by himself slowly, with Tom and Pierre behind him cheering him on. And even though he wished they wouldn't do that, he had a feeling he'd miss the cheering when he was back out in the world on his own.

Sometimes Jay would squeeze his eyes together and search inside the darkness of his head and it was almost as if his dad, always vigilant, could sense that Jay was trying to take himself back to the day of the injury in an effort to summon memories that might fill in the gaps.

'Hey, Jay, it's OK. Calm down. They say if you can't remember by now, you probably never will. It doesn't matter. Much better if you stop trying.'

It took a lot of hard work and discipline to learn to walk straight and properly again and during this time Jay's scar changed from a livid puckered red

band to a paler thing. It was still obvious and visible –
Jay had to accept that it would always be. But in
the end it had faded to something more like a wide
pink ribbon.

There would still be exercises to do after leaving
hospital, but he was young and strong, everyone
kept saying.

Jay had done what Pierre had pleaded with him to
do. He'd called on his invisible inner strength day
after difficult day. It wasn't long before he could walk
tall on the treadmill with Pierre and the rest of the
medical team praising and clapping from both sides,
as if he was breaking a record.

The morning he began to jog, just a little, and
only to see if he could, they called for Marie-Bernard
to come and see, and she wiped tears away with the
frilly end of her apron. Everyone in the room high-
fived him and then each other. Pierre said that this
was the most important moment of his medical
career. Jay realised all of a sudden that his body
felt different, stronger and straighter. Nothing hurt
any more.

They were going to keep him for one more week.
As soon the last checks were done, and as soon as
Pierre had signed him off, he and his dad would be
able to go.

There was cheering and whooping, and Marie-Bernard brought a cake with JAY NO 1! written in chocolate on the top. And everyone hugged everyone else, making Jay feel bad for not being quite as excited or happy as the rest of them seemed.

Surrounded by so much hope, he didn't have the heart to admit how scared he still was. And though the pain was gone, his body still didn't feel fully right. He wanted to tell everyone that he was not better. Part of him wanted to stay at the hospital.

He hadn't talked to his friends in ages, and now he was nervous about that too. What would he say when he saw them. Especially since he wasn't allowed to tell them the truth. And what would they say to him?

He wished everyone would stop saying how great it was for him and his dad to be getting back to normal. As far as he was concerned, he didn't feel normal, and he didn't look normal, and the life he remembered before the shark seemed far away and foggy and long ago – a place that he could never go back to.

He would miss a lot about hospital too. In that last week everything felt like a party. Pierre and the team of nurses and doctors cracked jokes, ruffled his hair, brought him basketfuls of presents. He was allowed to stay up late with the night staff and watch movies.

But on the night before his discharge Jay woke with a jolt, his heart galloping in his chest. He opened his eyes wide and looked at the wedge of pale electric light that came in through the glass panel from the corridor. He did not like this random feeling of panicked fear that had risen up in him. But, he supposed, even if his brain didn't remember being bitten by a shark, his body was keeping the score, reminding him from time to time of the shock and terror he had endured.

'We store trauma inside our bodies,' Lonnie had once observed. Jay hadn't understood at the time, but now he reckoned this was what she'd been talking about.

His dad gave Pierre a framed picture of Jay smiling and upright. It had been taken in the rehab room one day not long before. And he brought flowers and chocolates for the other nurses and doctors and a cheese voucher for Marie-Bernard (who did not care for sugar and was allergic to flowers). For Lonnie his dad had brought a book of poetry. And in the chaos of tearful goodbyes everyone hugged everyone else. Jay wished he could stay but at the same time wanted to go, and was half sad and half glad when he and his dad finally did.

If he could return to the club, the water, his snorkel, his surfboard and Louis, he might have some chance of feeling more like himself again.

'You and me are going to make a whole new start!' his dad kept saying.

'What do you mean?'

'It means we're leaving France. We're going to Ireland.'

'What? When?'

'Straight away.'

'Really? Like on holiday?'

'Yep! A long holiday. Maybe for good. Who knows?'

It turned out that his dad had been planning this from the start, making a ton of new arrangements from his phone. It would have been wrong of Jay not to be grateful. His dad kept reminding him how he'd been begging to go to Ireland for years. But now it was happening so fast and bits of the plan were confusing. Dad was soon scheduled to hand the keys of their apartment to their landlord, Pascal.

'But where will we live when we come back?' Jay tried to keep the anxiousness out of his voice.

'Oh, we'll have plenty of options,' his dad replied, swatting the question away as if it was a trivial thing. 'Pascal's place was getting too small for us anyway. We're both due a change for the better, don't you think?'

Pascal used to call their apartment the *garçonnière*, which made Jay feel like he and his dad were cool, two boys together, doing manly things, like fishing and paddleboarding and barbecuing and surfing.

From that apartment he had always been able to see the foam and glitter of the sea. He thought about the *garçonnière*'s red-painted doors, and the hooks in the cloakroom, and the long cubby where they stored their boards, and the shelves in his room, and the pictures on the walls. He hadn't seen any of it for so long. And now he wasn't going back there at all.

'Don't worry about anything, buddy. I'm having our stuff shipped over.' This made Jay feel more rushed and puzzled and worried than ever, though he knew it would have been unkind to complain, considering how hard his dad had worked to make this happen.

They took a taxi from the hospital straight to Pascal's. Jay waited in the taxi with the window open, breathing in the spring air and the nutty-sweet frangipane smell and feeling the bright salt-sting of the sea he'd almost forgotten. Pascal came to the window and reached in and patted Jay's shoulder, and Jay smiled awkwardly, though he didn't really feel like smiling. Pascal's handshake left finger marks on his dad's skin. Jay pictured his loft room full of his stuff, and the outdoor firepit and their fishing rods and his paddleboard and his surfboard and felt another sudden wave of deep sadness, and thought after all that maybe it was better there hadn't been time for one last look.

'Right, done! It's all systems go!' Dad said, full of energy.

Jay wasn't able to tell his dad that he hated the new plan. What about his friends, this coast, that ocean? Everything he knew? He couldn't visualise this fresh adventure in Ireland that his dad was so happy about. Dad's will was firm and purposeful, and Jay knew he didn't have a choice; this was happening because of him and for him. He begged his dad to take him down to the surf club to say goodbye to everyone. When they got there, the place was empty.

'Did you tell them we're going away?' Jay asked.

'Yep,' replied his dad, 'but they must be busy. Other stuff on, you know?'

'We're leaving the country and nobody can even be bothered to come and see us off?'

Tears wobbled in Jay's eyes. There was a hot-marble

catch in his throat. Then there was a rustle and a click, and someone sauntering out from behind the sheds. It was Louis, a cloth dangling from one hand and sandpaper screwed up in the other. He'd been sanding the boards, a favourite thing of his. At the sight of Jay he dropped the cloth and sandpaper and started running towards him in a way that made Jay wish he had more time, and that he wasn't crying.

'Jay. *Alors!* Jesus!'

While he was glad to have this glimpse of his friend, Jay was embarrassed by his own emotions and could only look at the ground. His dad stood between them the way you might protect someone from something dangerous like a snarling dog or a fast-moving missile, even though it was only Louis.

The talk was fast and garbled and Louis just about managed to tell Jay how sorry he was about what happened to him, but it was awkward and difficult to have a proper chat, because Jay's dad kept interrupting loudly and uneasily, saying they had to go, and promising that they would text or email in a few days.

There had been so much to say but, in the end, in that tiny slice of time they had, none of it could be said. And by then the rush for the airport was critical. Jay and Louis had always told each other everything, but they seemed like strangers. Even Louis's voice was different. He spoke in that slow way someone does when they think you don't understand their language.

Dad was the one who'd quickly explained the Ireland plan and, on hearing it, Louis put his hands on his hips and bent his head to stare at the ground too and then looked up again. 'So you're leaving? Leaving France? For Ireland? For good?'

'Not sure, maybe, we'll see,' replied Jay's dad, who by then had taken over the conversation.

'You'll come back to visit, though?'

'Ah, yeah, definitely, we will, of course, *bien sûr.*'

'And can we stay in touch?'

'Of course we can,' said Jay's dad, again looking at his watch.

'How are you feeling, Jay?' asked Louis in the back-to-front way of a time-pressured discussion. 'I mean, are you better?'

'I am,' said Jay. 'I'm fine.'

'You look it.'

'Thanks. I lost my phone, but I'm getting a new one and Dad has your number, so I'll give you a call, OK?'

'Do, don't forget. As soon as you get there. We'll talk properly then.'

'Yeah, we will,' said Jay.

'Come on, Jay, we must hurry,' said his dad.

There are small moments in life when people stand still and wordless and listening, as if waiting for something to be revealed, and so it was for Jay that day. It happened in an instant, just before they turned towards the taxi.

It was the sound of the sea slapping on the sand and the sight of the shimmer-wobble of the water that brought something important back to Jay's mind: the scream of that voice, high and hysterical, soaring above the roaring engine sound.

Jay, Jay, Jay, Jay, Jay, Jay. The voice had been much higher and shriller than his dad's. The bad thing about the voice was the fear in it. The good thing was he was now sure about something. He was sure it belonged to his mother. The memory of her words landed on him strong and sure: one more piece of the broken jigsaw.

For a few seconds Jay couldn't breathe, but there was no time to talk about it and no permission because of the rules his dad had laid down, and anyway they had to go. He did not know how he might begin this conversation now that even the simplest of subjects felt knotted with new complications. And the pain in his body that he thought was gone came back to him then like a drumbeat, a distracting background to this clumsy farewell, and it seemed to get worse as he climbed into the taxi and tried to arrange himself on the creaky seat.

Louis stood with his back to the glittering sea, his hand shielding his eyes in a way that made it look like he was saluting his friend.

Jay's head was a jumble of thoughts in the middle of which a new idea was blaring, very loud: his dad had told him that his mother had never shown up. But now Jay was positive he'd heard her there, somewhere near, screaming his name. And if that was true, then it meant his dad had lied.

CHAPTER 6

JESS

Bonnie Gillespie wore a luminous pink T-shirt, bright white shorts and stood on one foot out of the rain under the canopy beside the chipper, with the other tanned leg held up underneath her, like a flamingo. A yoga pose probably. She looked at me for a second, her face hard, full of pity.

Cian and Jimmy Bannon were in charge of their dad's ice-cream truck that morning and were blasting out music from inside it. They always did that, as soon as the smallest sniff of warmer weather arrived. They cleaned the spring salt off the truck and faced the sliding doors towards the sea and the van flashed like silver as they opened it wide to the world.

I saw the two of them spot me and then look away, and I got a small pain in my chest remembering how great it used to be to see them in the days when we used to be friends.

It wasn't so long ago that I'd been part of that gang: Cian, Jimmy, Bonnie, Ciara, Nick and me, but last year everything went wrong and I got kicked out. There hadn't been any formal ousting or anything. It was just that whenever I rocked up to hang out with them, they all got up and left. I'm not stupid. I got the message. I wasn't going to beg or apologise. I might have lost all my friends in some overnight upheaval, but at least I still had a few shreds of self-respect.

It all started when I told Nick that Bonnie liked him. To be honest, I thought I was doing Bonnie a favour, and poor Nick wouldn't have had a clue. I had the mistaken idea that Bonnie had *wanted* me to tell him. At least that's what I'd taken from the conversation we'd had. But it turns out that, as far as Bonnie was concerned, the whole thing was a deathly secret, which confused me too. 'If it was a deathly secret, then why did you tell me?' I'd asked her, and she'd laughed a weird mirthless laugh and said, 'Exactly! I've learned my lesson with you, Jessie, and I'm never telling you anything ever again.' She said me blurting it out was a sign of extreme disloyalty. I said it couldn't have been a secret because I knew it even before she'd told me. Everyone in the whole town knew except for Nick, so the only thing I'd done was say a blatantly obvious thing to Nick, a thing he had a right to know according to the principles of freedom of information. But Bonnie didn't accept any of this and kept on behaving as if I'd broken the Official Secrets Act. In the courtroom of friendship I had no defence and, as is the law in Cloncannor, once Bonnie took a dislike to me then I was automatically banished by that whole crowd, and abandoned to the cheerless fate of solitude. The whole thing had been very unfair.

I stood so close to Bonnie that she couldn't ignore me any more, but hers was a cold hello and so was the hello I said back.

I was glad Davy was with me. His faithful company made me feel less humiliated. Still, I didn't want to hang around.

When we'd strolled down the road and past the corner where no one could see, I gave Davy a lick of my cone. But bumping into them had shaken me and I needed to calm down before facing my family again, which is why I decided on the long way home by the old cottage where I used to play.

I hadn't been since last year on account of it being another place I was banned from. But, unlike the sea, where everyone could stare at me from wherever they happened to be along the bay, especially the front room of our house, the old cottage was a brilliantly private hidden place. It's why I loved it so much. It might have been broken down and a bit hazardous, but it was mysterious, and I could stay there for ages and no one would know and therefore not be able to annoy me.

According to my family, people who played anywhere near there were doomed to suffer painful and horrific deaths. If they'd ever found out how often I'd ignored the warnings, they'd all be dead now from shock or a stroke or heart attack.

The cottage had always been at the edge of our land, on the wild side, not visible from our house on account of being at the bottom of the hill nearer the north bay of Cloncannor Beach. I used to be afraid of it, the way many people are afraid of old empty buildings where no one has lived for years. Gradually I'd gathered the nerve to approach it, and to run down the hill and sit looking at its rickety tumbledown shape from a distance. And each time I visited it, I'd get a little closer, until one day I tiptoed up its broken path and through the doorless frame of the main entrance. I remember the thrill of crashing through the huge cobwebs that had been spun by busy spiders in the corners and across the windows. There was a gaping blackened fireplace in a room that I guessed must once have been the kitchen.

Underneath the rubble in another room, I'd found an old mattress, rusty springs curling out of it. I let the gang in on my secret place, although now I wish I never had.

Last year, when the lot of us were there together one day, in some wild, illogical mood, Nick and I decided to drag the mattress out on to the bumpy ground at the front even though Bonnie and Ciara kept telling us to stop. The two of us lay on it then, laughing and looking at the sky until Bonnie got an asthma attack and Jimmy and Cian said we'd all better go with her to my house in a hurry for help.

Hay fever, we said it was, hoping not to be found out, and my mother narrowed her eyes and peered at us all. 'Hay fever? Sure, this isn't the season for that. The pollen count is at an all-time low. It isn't hay fever she has,' Mam said. 'It's something else.' For a second I'd thought Bonnie was going to shop us, but she didn't. In the end, Bonnie's parents had to go to Doctor Crilly and Bonnie had to get a nebuliser and that was when I'd told Nick that Bonnie liked him. But the next time I called to Nick he said, 'Look, Jessie, I don't think we should go down there any more,' and I was like, 'Ah no, come on, it's our secret place,' and when I called to Bonnie, she was like, 'I don't really want to,' and Jimmy, Ciara and Cian agreed. I said, 'We can stay away from the mattress,' and Bonnie said, 'Jess, it's not about the mattress. It's got nothing to do with that. It's about you and your big blabbermouth.'

I tried to explain, but Bonnie did not want to listen and since everyone stopped talking to me after that the only option available was to stop talking to them, and that's basically how my life as a loner began.

After the big falling-out I returned to the cottage by myself a few times, glad at first that I didn't have to worry about the rest of them any more, because of how fussy they were and because of Bonnie's asthma. But somehow my new reclusive status had taken the magic away from the place and it didn't feel enchanted or exciting. I ended up kicking a few jagged cans around the floor and picking up some of the stone from the broken wall outside and breaking it into rocks and firing the rocks towards the dunes. That was the last time I'd been down there, about six months ago.

So a visit was definitely long overdue. I didn't need any of them. I liked that the old place was my secret and that it was waiting for me. I could feel it drawing me back suddenly and powerfully, like a magnet.

CHAPTER 7

JAY

In the taxi, Jay stared at his dad as they sped towards the airport and he listened with a new alertness as his father chatted away in French to the driver. Jay watched where the edges of his father's eyes crinkled when he laughed.

'What?' asked his dad, noticing the change in Jay. 'What is it? Are you OK?'

'It's nothing. I'm fine,' Jay replied, even though he wasn't fine.

His dad was the person he depended on, the one he believed in. But it seemed that he had turned into a stranger too. Why would he lie to him? Why would he even have wanted to? As they arrived at the departure terminal, Jay grew more convinced that there were facts his dad was covering up, information he was leaving out, details Jay needed to know.

He kept these thoughts to himself, putting the remembered sound of his mother's voice – precious and frightening – in a dark corner inside him, along with everything else.

Jay had wanted a new set of earphones for the flight, but obviously earphones were a touchy subject with his dad, so he made do with a book. The engines screamed and whistled and whirred as the plane zoomed along the runway. Everything rattled. Everything shook. He'd been on a few flights in his life and he'd never been scared before, but he was scared now.

He disliked this new nervous version of himself and didn't want his dad to notice, or to worry, so he managed to calm himself with the breathing exercises he'd learned from Lonnie.

He began to relax a little when the seat-belt signs went off and the captain made her cool, friendly, cheerful announcements about the cruising altitude and the clear view. He was distracted, though, by the weirdness of being up there in the neutral sky, away from the home they were leaving and not yet near the home they were going to.

His dad read the paper, lowering the pages with a

rustle every so often to ask Jay if he was OK. Jay kept saying yes but by then his suspicions had grown unendurable.

This was it, he decided. This was the right time. Here would be the perfect place.

'Dad,' he said softly, half afraid of the question he was about to ask.

Fully hidden behind the paper, at first it seemed as if his dad hadn't heard.

'Hey, Dad! I really need to talk to you.'

'What is it? What do you need?' Dad looked up and down the aisle as if he was about to get the attention of one of the air stewards. 'They have water or juice. You can even have a Coke if you like – a treat in honour of our new start.'

'I don't want a Coke, Dad. I'm fine for drinks. I just want to talk to you. It's important.'

'OK, right, I see.' And slowly Jay's dad folded the paper and looked carefully at his son. 'Well, then. Fire away.'

'I need to ask you one more thing about Dellabelle Cove.'

'Jay, lookit, we've been through this. You know the deal.'

'I know, but I'm not going to talk to anyone else, just you. And it's only one question – and it matters a lot. I'll never say another word about it if you just tell me this.'

Jay's dad said he couldn't argue with that.

'You said Mum didn't show up, but I've been thinking about it and the thing is, I'm almost sure she was there.'

'Why do you think that?'

'There are things that have come back to me, things I can remember now. After my earphones fell off I know I could hear you shouting, but there were two other sounds. I sometimes hear them in my head now, or in my dreams. One is the sound of an engine somewhere above me. The other is a voice, a woman's voice.'

Dad held on to the arms of his seat. 'Go on,' he said cautiously.

'Well, there had been no one else there when we arrived, and we'd arranged to meet her and she'd promised to be there. I'm sure that voice was Mum's – screaming my name over and over again. And if it's a dream or a wish, then that's OK, but I can't stop thinking that she did show up, that she *was* there, that she must have seen me, and, Dad, please, if it's true, then I need you to tell me. I need to know.'

Jay's dad seemed to brace himself and could not look Jay in the eye.

'I'm sorry. You're right,' he said at last, and to Jay's great relief his dad seemed about to confess.

'I haven't told you the whole story. I was hoping not to have to tell you for a while. It's bad, Jay, but since you've asked me straight out it would be wrong to hide it any longer.'

At last, thought Jay, *here it comes. Here comes the truth.*

'I wanted you to recover first, you see. Build up your strength before telling you. It would have been too much to take on in one go. You're right. That voice you remember – it *was* hers. Jay, you see . . .' Jay's dad was coughing now.

'What is it, Dad? Are you OK?'

'Yeah, I just need a minute.' His dad took a few sips from his water bottle and spoke again. 'She jumped in, you see, to try to rescue you, and the truth is . . . I can't say it . . .'

And right then, Jay made a sudden decision. Just as he knew his father couldn't stand to say it, he knew he couldn't stand hearing it either.

'Don't, Dad, it's OK. Don't say any more.'

He'd heard enough.

His mother had died trying to save him from the shark. That's what had happened. She *had* come. He knew it. He'd heard her in the water. It made horrifying sense. She'd come, and she'd rescued him. He was a strong swimmer but he'd known there was something odd about the story he'd been told. There's no way he'd have been able to get away from a shark on his own, not without help. No wonder his dad couldn't say it. His mother had sacrificed her life to save him.

'We never have to talk about it again,' his dad was saying, as Jay's tears swam down his face and off his chin.

'It's OK, Dad. I'm sorry. We never will. I promise we never will.'

They hugged each other, both knowing that an oath of silence between them had been made.

Jay wondered if there'd been a funeral but knew he couldn't ask. He wasn't sure what he felt. It didn't feel like grief. It didn't even feel like sadness. How can you be sad about something you have never had? How can you grieve for someone you don't remember? It was more like blankness or emptiness. Like his whole life he'd been holding on to a thin pencil sketch of her, this tiny flicker of hope. Not only was he was going to have to live with the thing that had happened but he'd also have to let her go now, stop clinging – as he had done – to a promise that could no longer be kept.

Jay wasn't angry with his dad any more. He realised how hard it had been for him to admit what had really happened. But he was glad the truth was out. He knew the worst now.

He thought he'd been so cool, fighting off the shark, battling for his life on his own in the water, but it wasn't true. He hadn't fought the shark. His mother had done it for him. And now she was gone.

It was a good and terrible thing that he finally knew this. Good, because we must always know the full story of what has happened to us, and terrible for the obvious reasons. Jay was going to have to be tough. He was going to have to fend off the guilt. That would be the hardest bit. The thought that she had been near, that she had finally been within his reach, and that he had been the reason she'd died. He understood how much his dad had wanted to protect him from that awful fact.

'Is there anything else you'd like to know?'

Jay said no, there was nothing, and his dad looked relieved and exhausted and soon fell asleep.

Jay stared for a very long time out of the window, looking down at the candyfloss clouds. The plane was speeding forward, many, many miles a minute, but up here his senses were deprived, and there were none of the landmarks or signals he normally relied on to help him understand direction or movement.

For a while it felt to Jay as if they were hovering or holding still in the middle of a shocked nowhere.

There was no one else to blame, no one else to be angry with, no one else to rage at. He told himself that he must not cry any more.

The seat-belt signs pinged on. 'Fifteen minutes to landing. Fifteen minutes to landing,' announced the captain.

'Now starts our new story, our new life,' said his dad, waking up. 'We will leave the damage behind. We will start afresh.'

'But how will I explain this? Jay said, pointing with his good hand at the scarred side of his body. 'What will I tell people?'

'Buddy, you're getting better all the time. You're walking so well again now. Pierre said that as soon as you're back swimming, you'll be fully better in no time. He said to get in the sea as soon as you can. Not to let too much time go by.'

'But if I swim, people will see my scars, and if they see them, they'll ask what happened, and if they ask, then what am I supposed to say?'

'You don't understand,' his dad said. 'This is Ireland we're talking about. People wear wetsuits year-round. It's not like the south of France. It's nothing like Dellabelle Cove or the surf club or anywhere you're used to. It rains all the time here. And no one ever talks about their feelings and no one makes personal comments about what may or may not have happened to other people.'

If he was trying to make Jay feel better about their new start, it wasn't the greatest of advertisements. An emotionally stunted place where it never stops raining? *Great*, he thought, *just what I need*.

'The point is, Jay, you can cover it up. Nobody needs to see or know anything. And if someone does happen to see, they won't ask, and if they do ask, you don't have to answer, and nobody will think there's anything wrong with not talking about it. It's all going to be OK. You're going to recover from this.'

But as the plane touched down in Shannon airport with a stutter of sickening jolts, Jay wasn't sure if he would ever recover. Not from the pain that still lurked inside him, ready to attack at unexpected moments, not from the broken promise of his mother. Not from that hope of knowing her at last. Not from the image of her facing the shark to win the battle for his life and lose the fight for hers. How close the possibility of a sparkling normality had been – just within reach – and then in one moment it was gone for ever.

CHAPTER 8

JESS

I reached the crest of the far hill and looked down towards the cottage. Around it a new and different light seemed to shine. The roof twinkled and the windows glinted and flashed on and off like a lighthouse. Davy loves a good sprint. Something suddenly seemed urgent, so we started to run.

We followed the twisted path whose smoothness gave way to the tufty spongy ground by the dunes. Davy's paws thumped and pattered. I love it when Davy runs, with his tongue hanging out of one side of his mouth and the way he looks like he's laughing. Both of us were out of breath and panting when we got to the bottom of the little valley where the cottage nestles. It wasn't until we were very close to the front door that it hit me. The reason the cottage had seemed to be shining and glinting in the sun was because it *was*.

I stood for ages before making sense of it. The whole place was clean and fixed and lovely: a new candy-apple-red door with a stained-glass fish leaping in the middle and the blanched-dazzle white of the walls, and the smoothed-out garden with the rocks and bumps and tufts replaced by bright shiny green and soft floppy-blossom flowers, and a velvety lawn and a fence. And a field full of straight rows of growing things. How could this have happened without me even knowing?

I stared for ages at the neat restored loveliness that used to be my secret ruin. I shouldn't have been surprised. My family never tells me anything.

Davy looked amazed too. He and I tiptoed round by the side wall where there was now a designer meadow filled with a flock of multicoloured flowers. Still baffled, we wandered to the front again and gaped, our mouths open at the perfect lawn that someone had laid and rolled like a velvet carpet. On either side of the freshly painted door were hanging baskets full of white daisies and pink lilies. I noticed the sign then – high up on the stone wall. SALE AGREED.

My parents had renovated and sold the place. A fence marked out the new boundary. Davy looked concerned, staring deeply at my face, with his head tilted to one side and then the other.

I cupped my hands at the glass and peered in. There was a marble top on a newly installed kitchen, gleaming cleanly, and two orange sofas in the front room and a new matt-black stove where the old stained hearth used to be. In another room a big bed with a brand-new, clean, cloud-thick mattress and no sign of the ancient one anywhere and nothing broken and everything looking like an ad in a magazine. The place was so well locked up and secure that I'd have had to break something to get inside, which I decided against.

'Come on, Davy,' I said. 'Nothing for us here any more. I guess we should go.'

Davy and I were too tired to run, so we trudged back up the twisted lane. Davy stayed beside me the whole way home, extra close. I decided I wasn't going to say a word to Mam and Dad about any of this. I was going to maintain a dignified silence. I mean, that was my plan, until I saw them.

'Why didn't you tell me you were doing up the cottage? Why didn't you tell me you were selling it? I can't believe you kept that a secret.'

Dad said they hadn't done anything in secret, and asked what did I think the cement trucks were for last winter, and why it hadn't occurred to me to ask the team of builders – who came in every day for months, for tea and sandwiches – what they were doing?

'How could I have known unless someone told me? Like was I supposed to *guess*? People drop in here for tea and sandwiches the whole time.'

'You should be glad. We'll have neighbours. They're due to arrive today. The new owner sent advance gardeners and planters three months ago and now there's a big field of vegetables, already ripe for picking.'

'I know, I saw it.'

'Peas, broccoli, rhubarb, cabbage, cauliflower, carrots, spinach, asparagus, chard, lettuce. A field full of riches. He applied for a licence at the farmers' market. It's just been approved. Love that. A man who plans ahead. Ready to hit the ground running as soon as he gets here. I'll be dropping round in the morning to say hello. Why don't you come?'

'No, you're OK, thanks, Dad.'

'Right then, suit yourself. I'll make sure to keep you posted.'

'That'll be a first,' I replied.

CHAPTER 9

JAY

By the time they were in the passport queue Jay had absorbed the truth about what had happened and knew it was something he was going to have to try not to think about, and never discuss.

He couldn't get her out of his head, though. He'd spent his whole life doubting whether his mother cared about him. At least now he knew she did, and, not only that, that she was a hero. She'd faced the greatest of dangers. She'd fought and died for him. What more could anyone do to prove their love for someone?

He thought about her courage and her steel and the great love. The guilt was so powerful it was glowing in him now. But he was proud too. He would never know her reasons for staying away, but he could never now say she'd abandoned him. Not

when she'd appeared like an angel to save him –
there when he'd needed her most. These were the
thoughts that would get Jay through.

Thank you, Mum. Thank you for fighting for me.
Thank you for saving me.

He tried to imagine what she might say back
to him if she could: that he was the treasure of
her life and that she was happy to have done
what she did, and that she'd do it again a hundred
times over.

She had seen him, and she had seen the danger,
and she had made a fierce decision to fight with
every last gasp in her, and in that way she'd been
triumphant. She mustn't have hesitated for a
second, jumping into the teeth of the shark so Jay
could be saved. No one else had a mother who'd
done anything like that for them.

Once he'd hated her for leaving them and for
being so hard to contact. He'd never feel like that
about her again. No one could have loved anyone
more than she'd loved him.

It hardly ever rains in the south of France, especially
not in April, so when Jay and his dad trundled
through the exit doors at Shannon airport, there

was no mistaking the newness and the difference of this place. Jay watched the raindrops flipping like tadpoles on the concrete as they waited at the taxi line.

'Where are you headed?' shouted a large man – white shirt, mad curly hair.

'Cloncannor,' said Jay's dad.

'And you're getting a taxi?' said the man, scratching his head.

'That's what we were hoping,' Jay's dad replied.

'Bad plan,' the man said. 'They'll ride you for the fare. Name's Mattie Feeney.' He grinned at Jay and pointed to a dirty white minibus on the forecourt. 'That's my bus. Mine's the Dublin–Shannon–Cloncannor route. Twice a day. You're in luck. I'm headed to Cloncannor in less than ten minutes.'

Dad told Mattie he had himself a deal.

Jay felt dizzy and sick and disorientated, but there was no room to think the huge thoughts or feel the massive feelings, and no permission to talk about any of it, and maybe this was for the best. Thinking about the shark and his mother made a kind of bleakness swirl darkly inside him, weakening him again as if he was still fresh from his injuries.

'You've gone a bit pale, buddy,' said his dad. 'Let's get you settled. You can relax and take in the scenery.

Isn't it great to be here at last? All those petitions you used to mount? Your wish come true, huh?'

Jay said it was great, but secretly he wasn't that interested in looking at the scenery. If he was honest, he could barely remember asking his dad to go to Ireland or if he had, it had been a long time ago, back when he'd been a kid, and when Dad's stories had meant more to him than they did now.

Gently his dad held him by his good arm and led him up the steps of Mattie Feeney's bus and made sure he was settled, and Jay sat very still as his dad pulled the seat belt and clicked it into place. 'OK, buddy? Not too tight?'

'It's grand,' said Jay, silently hating how his dad obviously thought he was some kind of large baby.

'Look! Look at this wonderful rain!' said his dad as if introducing Jay to an old friend. Jay had always loved how they jumped from English to French all the time, like their own little maze of language, but almost as soon as they'd touched down, Jay's dad stopped speaking French.

His dad was up there in the front seat chatting away to Mattie in his rock-solid permanent English as if they too were old friends.

'Haven't been back for a long time,' he was telling Mattie.

Mattie nodded as if he understood.

Grandad Seanie's heart had been bad. Years before Jay was even born, he'd dropped dead in a field one day when he was herding cows. And then straight after that his granny had gone into something called a decline. You'd never have guessed they'd had a ton of money, not from the few photos his dad still had. But they did. And Jay's dad was their only child and he was the one who'd inherited it all. Money didn't matter that much to Jay's dad, but there was security in having it all the same. They'd lived a simple life in France and it had only been the two of them. Most of the money was still in the bank, which was a good thing because, as well as a new home, they needed equipment and special facilities to help Jay with his recovery.

All the way to Cloncannor Jay's dad remained restless and excited and over-vigilant, exclaiming at everything he saw in a round-eyed young-kid way.

'That's the exit for Dromoland Castle, right there!'

Jay glanced over at a great thick band of forest, not entirely sure what to say.

And a little later his dad called out: 'This is it! The turn to the coast! We'll be at Cloncannor much sooner than I guessed, on account of the fabulous new roads. There was no motorway the last time I was here.'

'Jaysus,' Mattie said. 'You must have been gone a long time, so.'

'Yes. Yes, I have been,' sighed his dad. 'A lot of water under the bridge, as they say.'

Jay could not look at the way his father's chin had puckered then and he wished he had not noticed that crack in his voice. A terrible knot of feelings seemed to bounce between them. Great claps of regret. Rumbles of sadness. Sparks of melancholy and uncertainty mixed with vague flushes of hope. Jay was not ready for any of this. So he'd stopped listening and pressed his forehead against the cool of the window, a blur of countryside whipping past.

Instead he thought about Lonnie, and tried to imagine what colour his feelings might be now. The grey-green of sickening shame. Shame that it wasn't him who had fought the shark. Shame that he was the reason for his mother's death. He was angry too, and it felt like that anger was boiling somewhere, a roiling, seething hot spring underground. Bursts of the wine-dark sea cracked back into his mind, glimpses of the pinkening foam and the thrashing water and his mother's voice calling out his name in horror and in fear.

*

Their new house was so close to the beach that little trails of sand formed in eddies on the flagstones bordering their new garden.

'Ah, the foam-edged Atlantic!' declared his dad. It was only then that Jay discovered all that had been done – the team of planners and builders who'd been working away to get this place in shape during Jay's months-long hospital stay. Dad had found the perfect home. He'd insisted on familiar designs and a bedroom so like the one in their apartment that it would make the change easier for Jay. He'd even paid for a huge field of vegetables to be tilled and sown, and now many of those vegetables were ready to be pulled from the earth.

It was all lovely, Jay had to admit, but none of it mattered to him as much as the sea did. He dumped his carry-on on his new bed and then he hurried out and down to the beach and looked across the bay at the good waves out there and felt the spray on his skin and breathed in a great salty breath and thought, *Well, at least there's this.*

Jay could see this new ocean from his new bedroom too. His father had shipped Jay's favourite belongings, his old shelves and his desk, and he'd painted the walls of his new bedroom the same colour as the walls of his old bedroom so that every time Jay woke up, he'd have the feeling that he was home.

On one side of the luminous kitchen was an archway into a small clean space full of exercise equipment. 'This is your gym! You'll be able to ramp up the training like Pierre said.'

'Wow, Dad, thanks. That's so great.' Jay weaved between the weight machine and pressed the digital screen of a new treadmill, and turned the pedals of the stationary bike.

Outdoors, at the back, there was a small pool called a 'rehabilitation tank' in which Jay would also continue to build up his strength, in case he wasn't quite ready for the sea. If you pressed the green button, jets of water created whirls of current. There were four settings: gentle, moderate, strong, very strong. Jay pressed, and stared at the water as it churned and bubbled, but he felt that sickness again and turned it off.

'So, what do you think?'

Jay had to admit that it was great – it all was – and he walked round slowly again, noticing once more the door and the flowers and the grass and the kitchen and the gym and his room with pale walls exactly the same colour as home. He liked that the window opened from the bottom so a rectangle of cool breeze drifted in and he could hear the wild, inviting whisper of the sea, and wondered when he would have the courage to get into it. There was a black blind that he could pull down to make the room totally dark, and a TV, and everywhere the smell of fresh paint.

Jay thanked his dad for all the trouble he'd gone to what with this new house and this new garden.

The pull of the sea was constant. Jay stood in the front garden. The short grass blades shone like lime peel. He looked at the hill to the left and the vegetable field to the right, and straight out at the sea again, listening to the waves lifting, rolling, tumbling, crashing on to the beach.

'That's ours too,' said Jay's dad, and for a second Jay thought he was talking about the ocean, but quickly realised he meant the huge field behind the stone wall, with neat rows and ridges.

'We're going to sell those vegetables at Cloncannor market. Our new venture!'

'Great, Dad, yeah, really good,' said Jay. Had they actually left France for ever? Was this a permanent move? It was starting to feel like that.

There was a pantry at the back of the kitchen for keeping dry goods, and steel racks for storing the herbs and vegetables after they'd been pulled from the ground. Upstairs, a sunroom with dormer windows showed a bigger slice of the sea view beyond the dunes, and there was a changing room at the back door Jay hadn't noticed at first: for their wetsuits and their togs and their fishing rods and flip-flops and visors and a surfboard or two.

'A surfboard?' said Jay. 'Did you ship our surfboards?'

Jay's dad said he'd left them behind. He'd told the club they could have them.

'It's time you got a new one. You've grown so tall.'

Jay shivered at the thought of this – a blend of sadness and hope.

There was a cosy living room with bright couches. This was the room they'd fill with books and music and where they'd keep another TV. There was a brand-new shining black stove. 'That's for the winter nights,' said his dad, 'but we don't have to think about winter for a while. Not with summer in front of us now.'

'And here – ' His dad was pointing. Outside the hallway by his bedroom there was a wooden door Jay hadn't noticed, with a black-painted latch that his dad lifted with a deliberate click and an ostentatious flourish of his hand, as if he was doing something very significant and grand. 'This here's going to be my studio.'

Jay followed his dad into the bright, echoing space. There were grey shiny flagstones on the floor. Light flooded in through four windows in the ceiling.

'We'll take a few days to get settled and then you can start school. Place is booked, they're expecting you.'

School? This was where Jay was going to draw a line. Starting in a new school with only a few more weeks to the summer holidays? In a place where everyone knew each other and he knew nobody? It was a step too far.

'Dad, there is literally no way I'm doing that. I don't care what arrangements you've made or what organising you've done, I'm not. I need some time. It isn't just about getting unpacked. I need to get used to it first. I've a lot to get my head around.'

His dad lowered himself on to a wooden stool in the hall. 'Of course you do, buddy. That's why I thought school would be just the thing! The perfect place for finding your feet. People your age. Structure. Focus. All the good stuff!'

But the certainty of his dad's voice had already begun to trickle away.

'Dad, please.' Jay gripped the handle of his new bedroom door. 'I'm barely holding on by my fingernails here. I've gone along with these gigantic changes. You can't make me go to school yet. I didn't know it was part of the deal anyway, and if you want me to go, OK, I will, but just not now. Not yet. After the summer is over – I'll think about it then.'

Jay walked into his new room and sat on the bed, feeling small. His dad came in and sat beside him. When Jay was little, if ever he was sad or angry about anything, his dad would always sit beside him and he'd ruffle up Jay's messy hair and quietly say, 'Hey, mate' or 'It's OK, pal' or 'What is it, buddy?' And those whispered words had always been enough to calm Jay down. For a moment he thought about that smaller, easily soothed version of himself and wished he could go back there, to a time when life was sunny and simple and no damage had been done and where hard memories and new trauma did not clash invisibly against each other and against him in this complicated air.

There was a loud three-tap knock.

'Hellooo? Ah, hello!'

'Someone's here,' said Dad, looking relieved and rushing towards the brand-new voice.

A man filled the doorway: green wellington boots; friendly, open face. 'Sean Flanagan's the name, great to meet you at last,' he said, shaking one of Jay's dad's hands with both of his. 'Welcome. Delighted to see this. When we started the renovation we never thought it could look so smart, but you've made it spectacular, given it a fabulous polish altogether. Finished it off wonderful, so you have!'

'Yeah, thanks, we're pleased.' All the soft French curves in this Dad's voice seemed to have gained harder Irish corners and edges. 'Aren't we, Jay?'

Jay was standing half in the hallway, half in his room, feeling clumsy and silent and stupid. Instantly he put his hand to his neck to cover the scar, not knowing how else to conceal it at such short notice.

'Hello there, Jay, and welcome to you too! The whole gang's looking forward to meeting you both. We don't want to be crowding you or anything but everyone's eager to say hello. So, listen, rather than landing in on you like a bunch of uninvited cattle, we thought you'd join us tomorrow night?'

Jay's dad became exaggeratedly delighted. 'Wow, well, OK, yes!'

'It's Cloncannor's annual spring gathering. Nothing posh. Just a general get-together on the beach here. Bonfires, barbecue, bit of music, bit of craic. Everyone wants you to know you'd be more than welcome.' Sean Flanaghan stopped and beamed at Jay and his dad. 'Honestly, delighted you're here. We never used this part of the land and the building was a ruin for as long as I remember. We couldn't be happier to see it get a new life. Our place is over the hill; just follow the path round to the left and up. Cloncannor Beach has two bays. The north one – straight ahead of you, and the south one, right next to it, that's where we have the surfing school. Just follow the signs, in case you're interested.'

'Now isn't that lucky?' said Dad. 'Jay will definitely be. He's mad about the surfing.'

'You're in the right place, so! Lessons every day through the summer. Will you be starting school above?' asked Sean, pointing off in a different direction.

'We were just talking about that, weren't we, Jay?' Jay nodded.

'Yes, he'll be going, but maybe not quite yet.'

'Ah, isn't that great?'

And Jay said, yeah, it was.

'Right then, I'll leave you to it and look forward to seeing you tomorrow.'

Sean Flanagan turned and then turned back again. 'Tell you what – give me your mobile there and I can keep in touch with you that way.'

'Actually, we left our mobile phones behind,' Jay heard his father say.

'Ah, dear that's a nuisance, but not to worry – you'll be able get set up with another one, no problem.

There's a mobile shop in Grangekellig town, only twenty K or so out the road. And if you need Wi-Fi installed, a pal of mine, Seamus Dooly's the name, is a great man for that: boosters, routers, woofers, tweeters, the whole lot.'

'Thanks, Sean, but we're not going to need any of that. We left them behind on purpose. We're planning to be a Wi-Fi free household. An uncomplicated life, that's what I'm after. Keeping it simple.'

'Sorry, Dad, what?' said Jay, but his father hushed him, while Sean Flanagan looked as if he was about to burst with a fresh wave of delight.

'Well, now, indeed, and isn't that great? And aren't you so right? I'd be all on for exactly the same myself – I mean, there's nothing I'd like more than to take the phones off my lot. Those gizmos and gadgets, the screens and digital whatnots, they're a curse. Attention spans of gnats my lot have. You're a better man than me, Patrick! Good on you. No phones. No Wi-Fi. That's some achievement these days.'

Jay slipped back into his room and pulled down the blind and flicked on the TV.

When he came out again, Sean Flanagan and his dad were still chatting away – in the garden now, both of them leaning against the wall. It seemed as if the two men were whispering.

'Excuse me. Hello?' said Jay, and they turned their faces towards him. 'In case there's any confusion, I don't need lessons. I'm already a surfer.'

'Ah, well, sure, even better. I'll look forward to seeing you out there in no time!' Sean pointed towards the sea as if Jay needed to be shown where it was. 'And see you tomorrow night! And don't be bothered about bringing anything! Just yourselves.'

When their new neighbour finally trudged back up the winding path, his wellies sending miniature avalanches of loose pebbles tumbling behind his heels, Jay's father looked at him and frowned. 'Jay, what the hell?'

'What the hell what?'

'It wouldn't hurt to make an effort. This is our new home. There was no need to bark at him like that.'

'I was only telling him the truth. Why would you say I needed lessons when I've been surfing since I was four?'

'I was being polite,' his dad said, pulling one of their suitcases along the ground through the hallway.

'And how come you're banning mobile phones? That's the first I've heard of it.'

Jay wasn't ready to meet a whole load of new people at a party but he didn't want to have a fight about that either, so the next time his dad mentioned it, Jay said, 'OK, fine, I'll go to that, but I'm not going to school. Not until after the summer.'

He hadn't wanted to wear the stupid scarf. That was his dad's idea, as well as the T-shirt with the long sleeves. The mark of the shark stretched wide and crooked from under his T-shirt and up past his jaw.

'But you said no one's going to ask any personal questions.'

'I did, and they won't. Still, we can't be too careful, not in these early days.'

Jay checked himself in the mirror, patted on a tiny bit of hair gel, did some of Lonnie's breathing exercises. His dad was in a hurry by then, standing in the doorway holding a bottle of wine in each hand. Silently they headed off under the fading light, along the path that curved towards the left and up the hill and over the dunes.

CHAPTER 10

JESS

Esme was still not talking to me and I was still not talking to her. And since I wasn't allowed to go into the sea any more, there was nothing to do except bring a cup of tea upstairs to my room and sit by the windowsill staring down at the bay. At least I could look at the ocean. There were no laws against that.

With my finger I traced Cloncannor Beach's capital B on my window, following the two curves of the north and south bays and the foamy line of the sea.

Next thing, there were footsteps creaking up the attic stairs and a knuckle rapping on my door. There's never any peace in this house, especially when I need it most.

'Come in,' I said. It was Dad, of course, looking delighted.

'Hey, get up, lazy!'

'I was up. I've made tea. I've come back to bed.'

'Don't you want to hear about our new neighbours? Aren't you curious?'

'What about them?' I said, sitting up like I cared.

'It's a man and his son.'

'How old?'

'My vintage, I'd say. Forty-five ish.'

Dad was always teasing me like that. I glared at him.

'Oh, sorry, you mean the boy? Exactly the same age as you. He'll be in your class! I've invited them to come along tonight.'

'What are they like?'

'Good. Very good. I think they'll make excellent neighbours. Your mother's going to be pleased about them. The boy's name is Jay. I didn't get a chance to talk to him much but he seems perfectly nice.'

Great, I thought, knowing from experience that my dad's version of 'perfectly nice' was not to be relied on.

'So if they come tonight, you're to make the boy feel welcome, right? Oh, and Jess, Patrick – the father – wasn't specific about it and said that it's not to be discussed, but I gather there was some accident, the boy's recovering from a trauma; I got the idea it was an injury. To be honest, he seemed thoroughly OK to me. No sign of a mother, though. Wouldn't dream of asking. So if they do come, just might be worth remembering they've been through some sort of hardship so be extra kind and give them space. Oh, and they've no mobile phones.'

I looked at Dad in baffled amazement.

'Yes, that's what I said. No phones. They're not even getting Wi-Fi. I've huge admiration for that.'

'Fabulous,' I said. 'A new neighbour with PTSD and no access to the Internet. Just what I need.'

'Jess, excuse me, but that is extremely unkind,' said Mam, bursting into the room, revealing without any embarrassment that she must have been lurking outside. 'And it's very unlike you and frankly you'd better snap out of this cruel mood or I won't let you go tonight.'

I was on the verge of telling her I didn't care whether I went to the party or not, but in the end I didn't bother.

When I was a kid, the Cloncannor Beach party used to make me sick with excitement, and even now, when I saw the four bonfires glowing along the south bay, and the fairy lights draped on the volleyball net and the candles dotted along the low wall, the old thrill shot through me. Everything seemed to blaze and crackle and it woke something up in me again. Maybe it was hope. Maybe it was magic. Anyway, it looked spectacular.

'Don't come down in those raggedy slides and make a show of us, Jess, do you hear me? Make an effort. Wear something nice.'

'Flip off, Mam, I'll wear whatever I feel like,' I muttered, so she couldn't hear. Davy and I would take our own sweet time, I decided. We'd wait for a while at least. Definitely until after Charlie's band had started playing.

I sat at my window watching as the evening began to take shape. Everyone looked tiny from there: miniature people, arriving and settling into the deckchairs and sprawling on the blow-up beds or sitting down at the picnic benches to chat and drink.

Dad, in charge of the barbecue, was flipping the burgers and I thought I could hear his big laugh even from this distance, and the crowd was thickening with people coming from every direction, some carrying folded-up deckchairs to set up on the sand, and others with boxes of beer for the grown-ups and bags full of giant marshmallows and popcorn for the kids. I could hear Charlie tuning up, trying the speakers, saying, 'One, teeooow, testing, one, teeoow. Can anyone hear me?' into the microphone.

'The whole of Ireland can hear you, Charlie!' I shouted out of the window, but I was too far away for him to notice.

By the time myself and Davy arrived, the light was trickling from the sky and it was raining again. Not that anyone in Cloncannor cared. They clustered in small groups under festivals of blooming umbrellas, their chatter mixing with the music, filling the beach air with sound. Cian, Bonnie, Nick, Jimmy and Clara were taking up half the beach, deep in the throes of two frenzied games of Spikeball. Jimmy whispered something, and then Bonnie, Nick and Cian started laughing uncontrollably.

I worked hard not to make eye contact with any of them and settled myself in one of the deckchairs furthest away. The tide was going out, and the broad damp strip of sand had a comforting coolness. I didn't care that no one came to talk to me. I preferred it, in fact. I was only there for one of Dad's burgers and the chance of a can of full-sugar Pepsi.

I prayed that nobody'd decide to drag me into anyone's conversation in some misguided effort to include me. I didn't want to be included, and I arranged myself in a way that I hoped made me look fully occupied, staring towards the water like I was studying something, and listening to the roar of the big surf that seemed especially wild. I dreamed myself out there on those forbidden waves.

I don't know what made me turn to look towards the dunes, but it happened to be at that exact moment that Jay Danagher and his dad came over the hill.

Like a miracle, the clouds had drifted away, it had stopped raining, and the sky was filled with stars. Jay Danagher and his dad were like gladiators. Tall, tanned, both with the same way of walking.

Jay was bundled up in a scarf and long sleeves like it was the middle of winter. The two of them moved in this slow, deliberate, cool way that made me instantly wish I was Jay Danagher's friend and suddenly hopeful I could be.

My parents swooped in on them with loud welcomes and enthusiastic hellos and introductions. I could hear Mam shouting for me, but for some reason I found I could not answer. In the end, they brought him over to meet me.

It took me almost ten seconds to struggle out of the low deckchair, which may not sound like a long time but actually is an extremely long time when someone's standing there looking at you, waiting to be properly introduced.

A warm blush seeped across me. *Don't act like an idiot, Jess*, I thought, straightening my leggings and smoothing my T-shirt. *Keep it calm. Try to be normal.*

Something happens to me in public, especially when I meet new people. Either my mind becomes instantly empty of all words and thoughts and I can't think of anything to say, or else I become overwhelmed with a massive muddle of concepts that I feel bizarrely compelled to share, in which case I literally have zero control over the things that come out of my mouth. I never know which it's going to be until the last minute. It's so nerve-wracking.

So it was a surprise that night when things between me and Jay Danagher began quite well. I said hello, and shook his hand. His dad and my parents wandered back over to a group of Cloncannor's adults who stood by the grill, swaying to Charlie's music. I offered to get Jay a Pepsi and he said yes please, and I told him to wait there and ran off and grabbed two cans and brought them back. I informed him my name was Jessica but that everyone called me Jess or Jessie, and he told me his name was Jay and everyone called him Jay.

So far, so good.

Maybe it was going to be all right. Maybe I wasn't going to sabotage myself.

Wrong.

It was only a matter of time before the idiot version of me came out of hiding. And, as luck would have it, she was on top of her game.

'My dad says I'm not to mention anything about your previous life, so obviously that's the first thing we should discuss.'

I'm not even sure what I was trying to achieve. Who knows? I think it might have been some feeble attempt at a joke. Needless to say, it fell flat on its face.

He looked at me as if he couldn't believe what he'd heard, and then he glanced around like he was afraid someone else had heard too.

'Sorry, but I can't tell you anything about my previous life. I'd prefer if you didn't ask,' he said, and his gladiator stance disappeared and he seemed to droop, as if he'd rather he was invisible.

'Okaaay,' I said, half wondering if this huge change in him was serious or if he was joking too. I waited for him to say something else but he didn't. 'Why can't you?'

'I just can't,' he said, looking at the sand.

'OK, fair enough, so in that case I'll stop asking.'

The music got louder and faster.

I started to dance – twirling around, gradually moving towards one of the bonfires, telling Jay to follow me, which he did, slowly and reluctantly, while the guitars and the drums and the fiddle and the keyboards rose to a firelit crescendo.

I danced in a huge circle round the fire and every time I passed Jay, who was standing there with his hands in his pockets staring into the flames, I whooped and said, 'Come on, Jay, loosen up. You'll like it – it's fun!'

Charlie held his low-slung guitar like a pro, and between each wildly smashed-out chord, he twirled his finger round his temple and threw a sympathetic glance in Jay's direction to let him know that even my own brother thought I was a bit crazy.

I couldn't help it. There's something in the strange bending light of a Cloncannor spring bonfire that puts me into a deluded state, which may have been why I thought there was still a chance for me to rescue the situation. I stopped my dance and approached Jay and tried again.

'Hey, look, I'm sorry. Honestly, I'm like a bull in a china shop; everyone says it. I mean, not that you're fragile or anything, and not that I'm actually a bull, but, like, it's just a metaphor. Oh god, sorry. Look, can we pretend I've just met you and I haven't said anything yet?'

Jay laughed a little bit then, which fed my hope.

'Yep.' He grinned, and his teeth were lovely. 'Happy with that suggestion. Give it another go.'

His voice was slightly Irish but mostly French.

'OK, great, hello,' I said. 'My name's Jess. I need to warn you: I'm a catastrophe, but, still, I hope we can be friends.'

He smiled and looked bashful and glanced down at my feet. In rebellion against Mam's instructions, I was wearing my oldest slides. The light blue nail varnish on my toes was badly chipped. Why had I not made more of an effort with my personal appearance, just like Mam had told me I should?

'So how come you're a catastrophe?' he asked, still smiling. He had these huge eyelashes and his eyes were green and I'd been staring straight into them for much too long, I realised, so I looked away.

'Where do you want me to start?'

'I don't know anything about you, so you could start anywhere,' he said.

That was the only encouragement I needed. 'OK, well, firstly then, as you've probably already figured out, I'm a social disaster. No one in my school even talks to me any more because of it. And I was supposed to become a surfer this summer but now that's not going to happen because of my controlling sister.'

'Sounds lousy,' he said.

Anything more I might have said about me went flying out of my head then and I stood there staring at Jay. 'So tell me about you. How are you?'

'I'm OK,' he said. 'I mean, it's been strange recently and this place is a big change, but I'm beginning to think I might like it here.'

And that's when I did it – I grabbed the end of his scarf. 'What's this for?' I asked. 'I know it's not the south of France but it's the warmest it's been all year. You don't need a SCARF!' I took the end of it and ran round him in circles, unravelling it. Then I froze. 'Wow' I said, 'what happened?'

The look he gave me then was fierce and frightening. He held his hand to his throat but he couldn't fully cover up the massive wide scar that was underneath. The party noise seemed to stop in one go, and my parents glowered at me and his father did too. A chill had drifted in from the sea like some old winter breeze had been lost out on the water and found its way on to the shore.

'What? What have I done?' I said.

Jay grabbed the scarf back off me, and messily bundled it round his neck again. He looked at his father, and his father growled something urgent at him and the next thing the two of them were saying polite thank-yous and leaving.

Jay didn't look at me again, let alone say goodbye, and honestly, if I'd had a spade, I'd have dug a massive hole in the sand and I'd have climbed right into it.

CHAPTER 11

JAY

'Jesus, Dad, what the hell? Why are we leaving?' His dad had grabbed him, telling the Flanagans they'd decided on an early night, and then he hurried the two of them back down the hill, in the dark, along the twisted path to the dim night lights of the cottage.

It had started so well. When Jay and his dad arrived at the beach, Sean and Annie Flanagan had given them broad-smiling, genuine welcomes and brought them round to say hello to lots of people whose names Jay instantly forgot.

It was an ancient Cloncannor tradition, Dad explained, and a nice coincidence that they had arrived in time for it. No one knew how far back it went, but Sean said his own parents and his grandparents and their parents before them had kept

115

it in their times, and it was as important to the village as Easter or Christmas or Halloween. The bonfires were to light the way for the ghosts of winter to get safely away on their sea journey and for the new ghosts of summer who were arriving. Or something like that. The main thing was it was a chance to get together.

Between snippets of conversation and introductions the Flanagans kept calling for Jess.

It was the sound of a barking dog that located her beyond the party lights and near the sea. She was lying back on a red deckchair outside the glow, as though there was a solitary bubble around her. She was tracing lines in the damp sand with her fingers as if she didn't even know there was a party on.

'There you are, Jess! Typical! Forever brooding at the water. Come on over here!'

It didn't seem as if Jess could hear.

'Oh, for goodness' sake. Honestly, that child never does what she's told,' said Annie Flanagan. 'Come on, Jay, let's take you over to her instead.'

Jess had messy hair, a funny smile, an excellent dog. She wasn't dressed up and she had no make-up on and she wasn't snooty or haughty or silent or scary the way strangers at parties often are. Even her feet were lovely. She stood up slowly. He liked the way she did that too, taking her time, not jumping to the tune of anyone else's instructions.

It's not often that someone really sees you the first time they meet you. Very few people see you properly at all, but Jess saw Jay.

There's a time in your life when you're not really supposed to dance. It's after you've stopped being a kid, and before you're old enough to get drunk. When you're thirteen, it's essentially the worst, most unthinkable thing you can do. Jess Flanagan had never got that memo. She kicked off her slides and she danced. She danced all natural, the way other people might drink water, or breathe, or laugh. The way she danced was full of truth and rightness. Jay couldn't stop staring at her. He hoped it didn't seem weird. And then, when gently she removed his scarf, Jay felt such a strange blend of relief and thrill that he thought he might cry.

Jess Flanagan had sensed his secret damage. She had something no one else had: the clarity to see his hurt, the grace to uncover it, the courage to ask him about it.

And in that moment, although it felt like she had broken a dark taboo, he realised just how much he did want to tell someone. She had known this. It was as if she had an extra sense. It would have been great if he'd been able to tell her. He knew he couldn't, though. He knew his dad was watching and so he should have known the moment wouldn't last. This was an impossible subject, and because of it the rest of the night was instantly ruined.

'Are you going to talk to me?' asked Jay when he'd been marched through the door. His dad was red-faced and out of breath and did not answer. 'Hey, Dad, I don't get it. First you drag me over the hill to a party I didn't even want to go to, and I do what you ask, and make an effort to talk to people like you said and everything's going fine, and then you drag me back here again. What are you trying to do? This isn't a great look for the new kid in town.'

His dad rubbed his face and scratched his forehead. 'Jay, look, I had no choice. I saw what that girl did. I heard what she asked. We can't be too careful. This is exactly the kind of thing I meant. I had to get you away from that danger.'

'Danger? Come on. We were only talking.'

'Why did she think it was OK to grab at your clothes like that? What did you tell her?'

'NOTHING, Dad. I told her nothing. Calm down.'

His dad lowered himself on to the couch and swiped his hand across his forehead and sighed a heavy sigh. 'Buddy, I'm sorry. Of course you weren't going to say anything. I trust you, and you trust me, huh? I overreacted; I think I'm tired. Maybe it's good that we left early. Maybe we could both do with some sleep.'

Jay opened his window before getting into bed. His secret felt like a prison again, and the blankness of his memory when he tried to think about it was a heavy chain weighing him down.

He peeled off the clothes that had covered him up, and slipped into the cool of his bed, tracing his fingers along the bumpy ridges of his scar. All the way from his neck down along his chest and his side and his leg. Then he stretched out under the covers. His body didn't feel so crooked any more, but the thoughts in his head were more contorted than ever.

His dad had been so sure that no one in Ireland would say a word, but his dad hadn't known about Jess Flanagan. She had only asked him what happened. She'd been full of decent curiosity and friendliness. She couldn't have known there was anything wrong about that. He'd wanted to answer. He'd wanted to keep talking to her, but now? Now he wondered if he'd ever talk to her again.

He stayed awake for a long time, listening to the mingled sounds of the ocean and the music and the trailing bursts of laughter that floated through the window from the party on the beach, and he wished more than anything that he was still there. He wished they were sitting on the sand together looking out at the sea towards the greater darkness. He wished she was telling him her secrets and he wished he could tell her his.

CHAPTER 12

JESS

The next morning I woke to the banging fear.

'Oh GOD! I hate myself so much,' I groaned, slouching at the kitchen table in my dressing gown, a mug of tea misting the space in front of me.

'What is it now?' Esme was making a smoothie, temporarily being nice.

'Last night!' I had to shout over the whizz of the blender.

'What about last night?'

'I was a total barge! I asked Jay Danagher all these personal questions that he didn't want to answer and then I took his scarf off him, and he was mortified, and he hates me now!'

'You don't know that,' Esme said, pouring deep blue sludge into tall glasses.

'I do know it. Did you see the way he looked at

me? Total scorn. He thinks I'm the biggest loser of all time. And, oh no, I asked him to *dance*! With *me*!'

'Did you?' said Esme, dipping a finger into her drink.

'Yes! Round the fire! Did you not see me?'

'Nope,' replied Esme, licking the same finger.

'You must be the only one. And the awful thing is, he had a *reason* for the scarf; it was covering a huge scar. Jay Danagher has a fabulous and mysterious past that he doesn't want to talk about! And I pulled his scarf off and stared at him and asked him what happened. I mean, who *does* that? I will literally never recover from the shame.'

'What did he say?'

'Nothing. Just shook his head and looked at the ground and said he couldn't talk about it. And in some crazy effort to pretend I wasn't embarrassed I had to keep leaping and hopping around the place like a muppet. Did you seriously not see me?'

'I did notice they left quite early. Everyone said it's because they've just arrived and still have to do all their unpacking and stuff,' said Esme, rummaging in the bread bin.

'It wasn't because of the unpacking. It was because of *me*! I've put him off me for life and I'll probably never see him again. Oh, Esme, why can't I just be normal like other people? What's wrong with me?'

'Where do you want me to start?' said Esme unhelpfully. By then I was almost crying from the distress of it.

Esme waited for the toast to pop, scraped both slices with butter and sat down at the table beside me. 'Hey, kiddo, come on. It's not all about you, remember? It mightn't have been you who scared him off.' She pushed a plate of toast and a smoothie in my direction. 'The whole of Cloncannor is a bit much when you meet us for the first time. Everyone says it.'

'You don't understand. He's the only interesting person who's ever come here and I've blown my chances of being his friend. I actually cannot bear to even look at myself.'

'Now you're just being silly,' said Esme, and she stroked my hair like I was a little kid.

'Yeah, enough with the drama,' shouted Charlie, who was out in the hallway packing the last of his stuff.

Dad stood by the door jangling his keys. They'd be late if they didn't go now.

'And, oh, nooooo, I forgot,' I wailed. I bent my head, resting my forehead on the flat of the table. 'Charlie's leaving today.'

Charlie, Mam and Dad came crowding into the

123

kitchen then, and I only had a few seconds to explain to Mam what happened.

'That's an exaggeration, I'm sure, sweetie,' she said, kissing me on the head. 'But always remember, for future reference, it's much the best thing not to ask personal questions of anyone. People who want to talk about themselves will do it anyway; they don't need anyone to invite them. And people who don't will appreciate not being prodded for information they have no wish to give away. Now stop making mountains out of molehills and hug your brother.'

There was a swoop of hugs and kisses and goodbyes.

'Bye, kiddo, be good,' said Charlie. 'You're going to have a great summer just as long as you don't do anything stupid.'

Esme and I stood at the door as my parents and Charlie climbed into the car. There was a hole in my stomach because Charlie would be in Spain until August and, though she was being OK to me in that moment, I knew I couldn't rely on Esme. Like the Cloncannor weather, Esme was volatile, always threatening to rain on my parade. To cheer me up, she made pancakes for lunch, though.

'You mightn't be so worried about the new guy in town when I tell you who I was talking to yesterday.'

'Who?'

'Your mate Nick. Nick Carmody.'

My stomach went cold.

'He's calling over tomorrow to find out about surfing lessons. Apparently he has a gang of cousins coming for the summer. So I'm expecting a surge in our numbers any day now.'

I didn't want to think about Nick and I definitely didn't want to meet him on our stretch of Cloncannor Beach, and the last thing I wanted was to see him surfing with my sister in the shallows or at the breakers or anywhere else, just so he could make a point of ignoring me. Now that I'd screwed up my chances of befriending Jay Danagher I was going to be a loner for ever.

Tormented, I sloped away up the narrow creaking stairs to my room and lay on my bed and squirmed at the horrible thought of the night before. In a small town like this you never recover from reputational damage, and mine was getting worse by the day.

I pressed my cheek against my pillow. Thoughts of Nick, Cian, Jimmy, Ciara and Bonnie – and thoughts of Jay Danagher – flashed at me like a broken movie, filling me with self-hatred.

Every time I was on the verge of sleep, some memory or other joggled my brain back into haunted wakefulness: Nick and me in that conversation from ages ago that I should never have had; Bonnie standing on one leg with her pitiless glare; Cian, Jimmy and Ciara at the beach party and the meanness of their laughter; and me dancing around Jay Danagher like some demented spring nymph in the flickering light of the bonfire.

I'd have to stay here in my room until I grew up, I decided, and then leave Cloncannor for good and never come back.

CHAPTER 13

JAY

In the days that followed, Jay's dad bought a car and furnished his art studio with tables and chairs and filled it with canvases, paints, stools, pots, brushes and the retro vinyl record player from their apartment in France. At night he began painting again to the sounds of Mozart or Queen or The Clash and sometimes this would wake Jay up and for a moment he would think he was back in their *garçonnière*. But he would hear the rain outside or feel the chill on his skin and remember then that they were far away from their French home. Wide-eyed in the cool darkness, he'd think about the old days, and how his dad had taught him paddleboarding and how to surf, and he'd remember the turquoise waves they'd caught together far away on a different shore.

Soon his dad had dug and pulled ripe vegetables from their new field. Physical tiredness was the cure for a great deal of stress, Dad often said, and brilliant for one's general state of well-being.

Jay worked on building his strength in the rehabilitation tank and the home gym. He wished he felt stronger and readier, but the inner tremble of his weakness made itself known in a hundred small ways. When he tried to help with the vegetables, just pulling them out of the soil could make him want to lie down for a while. The effort of getting in and out of the tank made him feel like an awkward, clumsy baby.

Every day, very early, he went for a walk along the shore, and wanted desperately to go into the sea, but he knew he wasn't ready, and, more than this, he was afraid, and afraid of admitting he was afraid. After the party had ended so badly, he felt more alone than ever.

He wanted to talk to Louis except anytime he even suggested getting a phone or Wi-Fi or a laptop, his dad would go on that anti-device rant again. Phones did not belong to his dad's vision of their new life. Jay would be much better off keeping at the gym and continuing his exercises in the pool. Or helping out on their new stall at the farmers' market. What could be healthier and more wholesome?

The Irish version of his dad was not like the French version. OK, sometimes he still whistled and seemed cheerful and happy, and when he did, Jay's sense of hope began to return. But at other times the darkness would settle like a huge crow landing on his father's shoulder.

Jay was learning new rules about what it took to keep his dad in a good mood. Don't talk about France or speak French any more. Don't argue. Don't ask questions about anything to do with the past. Never mention the earphones. Never ask for a phone. Don't talk about Dellabelle Cove or what happened to his mum. Keep his scar covered up. Definitely never mention the shark.

France felt like another planet now, though scraps of memory still came back to him from time to time. He remembered how he'd once got lost in a supermarket in Marseilles when he was small, and how his dad had fallen to his knees when he'd found him again. He remembered the smell of frangipane, nutty and sweet, from the bakery where he and his dad used to eat breakfast sometimes. And how cycling along by the coast you'd hit an invisible cloud that smelled like roasted almonds or lavender.

It's not that Cloncannor smelled bad or anything; it just didn't smell like France. He wondered if he'd ever again smell chestnuts or oysters or vanilla or proper French coffee. He remembered the loud bright colours of the Mediterranean and the way the French sunshine had spilled into his old room, sweet and liquid, like warm honey, and the sky's huge blue blankness. And his mouth watered when he thought about the oily mushroominess of the gigantic olives and the quenching juice of the fruits of France's south coast: pineapple, peach and pomegranate. He thought about how he'd promised to call Louis and how he never had, and how it was probably too late and how he wouldn't have been able to think of what to say.

He had plenty to do, but it was lonely work helping his dad, arranging vegetables by colour under the pantry's coolers and warmers and lights to create the perfect conditions for that shiny bumpy rainbow of fresh produce.

Jay woke early one Sunday morning to find his dad sitting at the end of his bed. 'C'mon, buddy, up. I'll need you today.' He hadn't wanted to go to the farmers' market but his dad had insisted, helping him get ready, watching him eat breakfast, making sure he wore his scarf. Jay did not look forward to the day, sure he'd feel as friendless and out of place as ever.

But he'd been able to carry four crates from the car to the stall with amazing speed and ease. He knew he'd been growing taller recently, and the way he could reach and lift the crates confirmed this. He was going to have to get new clothes.

He would have carried the rest of them, only his dad – who'd been busy introducing himself to the other sellers – noticed Jay and hurried over to wrestle the next crate out of his hands.

'I didn't mean that kind of help! They're too heavy.' They hadn't felt heavy to Jay. He knew he was growing stronger.

Business was brisk from the start. His dad twirled brown paper bags closed, making two little twists on either side like the ears of a small animal.

In pretty much no time Dad was in a happy rhythm, working fast to keep the queue moving, cracking jokes, throwing in free apples with the bigger orders. Jay was the one who felt like a stranger, odd and awkward in this wet, cold, rocky place.

At night Jay would lie on his new bed and stare through the window at the sky. Sometimes that sky was foggy with cloud, sometimes it was lit by a fat silver moon. He might not be allowed to talk about the accident, but no one could stop him from thinking.

In the private space of his new bedroom and from the darkness of his damaged memory Jay tried to see if he could summon the shark, but nothing would come to him, only those same random fragments. The sound of something shooting through the water, the blinding wallop of the attack, the plum-red blooming of his own blood; all those scraps of fear and shock like frantic flotsam come to torment him, bobbing to the surface.

The thoughts twisted around in Jay's sleep, merging into half-dreams. Noises too. The sound a bag of rocks might make if you grabbed it by the neck and whacked it off a wall; and sights like blood in the water and on the sand; and his dad's voice all gravelly saying, 'Christ. Jay. Christ. Jay. Jesus.'

Other things began to come back. He thought he could picture a helicopter and three men standing on the bloody sand looking out at the place where the attack must have happened. He thought he remembered the sound of a siren above him, or was that in his head? And then the feeling of lifting jerkily into the air and his dad telling him to cling on to life: 'Just hold on.' And something in his dad's voice grimmer than everyday fear.

He could also remember how on the way to the hospital his dad had said, 'You're the best boy a dad

132

could have. You're the miracle of my life,' and how hearing this had made him even more afraid.

These days he didn't feel like he was the miracle of his dad's life any more.

Even though he knew he wasn't supposed to, he raised the subject of the phone a couple more times, because of how much he wanted to talk to Louis. But it hadn't been worth the grief. His dad threw his arms up in the air, the way you might if catching a dangerous explosive thing.

'Can we please not start this again? We must both commit to settling in here, making this our home, right? So let's concentrate on that, shall we? And let's just keep moving forward.'

Of course Jay wanted to move forward. He didn't want to be haunted by the echoes of what they had left behind. And, yes, it made sense to make a new start – to get away from the place where it had happened, to begin again in a new world, on a new page with hope and with purpose. He couldn't argue with the logic of that.

The next time Jay helped with the stall, a boy with bright, hard blue eyes came strolling past. 'Hello,' he said, his hands in his pockets.

'Well, hello there!' said Jay's dad in this exaggerated friendly voice he'd only recently developed. 'And who are you?'

'Carmody,' said the boy. 'Nick Carmody.'

Jay's dad handed Nick Carmody an apple and when Nick rummaged in his pocket for some change, Dad said, 'No need! That's all yours. A present to you from us, right, Jay?'

Jay wished his dad had not dragged him into this ingratiating ritual.

'Thank you very much,' Nick said, sounding polite and grateful, and then he added, 'Are you the Danaghers?'

'Yes! Yes, that's us,' said Dad.

Shut up, Dad.

'Hey, well, in that case you're Jay?' Nick said, and his steely eyes glinted at him. 'I'm heading down to meet some friends for a game of pitch and putt. Would you like to come?'

'No. I mean, thanks, I'd like to, but I'm needed here,' said Jay, who was immediately betrayed by his father.

'Not at all!' said his dad, who claimed suddenly that he could easily handle the stall himself and was all delighted then, as if Jay going for a game of pitch and putt was the best idea ever.

'OK then,' said Jay, fuming, but cornered by politeness.

'Great, so!' said Nick. 'Follow me.'

They went down a back lane behind the market where there was a handball alley. Nick threw the apple against the wall where it smashed into lots of pieces that went spraying up in the air.

'Why did you do that?' Jay asked.

'Because I felt like it?' Nick replied.

'Yeah, well, it's not very nice,' Jay said.

'Yeah, well, I wasn't trying to be nice,' said Nick.

Not knowing what else to do, Jay followed him to the pitch and putt and Nick introduced him to four other people: brothers called Jimmy and Cian, and friends called Bonnie and Ciara. Bonnie was especially friendly and wanted to be paired with him. 'I've heard all about you!' she squeaked, which made Jay wonder what she'd heard or how she could have heard it.

Bonnie and Jay ended up winning the game, a fact that made Bonnie even more delighted than she'd already been. 'So what's your story? Like, are you on holidays here or what?' she asked.

Before Jay could say, 'I thought you knew all about me', Nick spoke on his behalf.

'He's moved here. Into the Flanagans' cottage.'

'The Flanagans' cottage?' Bonnie echoed. 'That old broken-down place by the beach?' She looked faintly disgusted. 'It's a ruin.'

'Not any more,' said Nick. 'It's been dickied up and refurbed and he lives in it now, don't you, Jay Danagher?'

'Yeah,' said Jay, gently kicking at a pebble on the path, wishing he could think of an excuse to leave.

'Next door to Jessie Flanagan? Oh, lord help us, poor you. Bad luck,' said Bonnie.

'What's bad luck about that?' asked Jay.

'Nobody likes her,' said Nick, as if this explained everything.

'I like her,' said Jay simply. 'I think she's great and so is her family, and I don't think it's unlucky to live next door to her.'

'Think what you like; it's a free world,' said Bonnie.

Then Cian and Jimmy, who'd barely said a word, started wrestling each other in a random way, and Bonnie and Ciara and Nick all did this identical snickery laugh, and by now Jay didn't care if it seemed rude to leave, because he couldn't have stayed there another single minute.

'How are you settling in?' said a beautiful woman one day, slowing in her car.

'Fine, thank you,' said Jay.

'Oh, good. My name's Judy Carmody. I'm Nick's mother. I've brought you a cake.'

'What for?'

'It's to welcome you to the town.'

Most mornings Jay trudged along the beach, even when it was raining, which was often.

The call of the sea was getting stronger. He had been afraid it would be one huge enormous trigger. But this sea was nothing like Dellabelle Cove. Sometimes it was gun-metal grey, sometimes a deep vivid violet, sometimes mermaid-green. Its surface could be stippled and soapy, or smooth, sometimes with a great swell rising from the far beyond. But not once in the whole time he'd looked at it was it ever like Dellabelle. Its sand was never sparkling hot-white, and it never burned the soles of his feet and the water was never the lurid blue Mediterranean kind. These belonged to his old world and to things of the past.

Anyway, it wasn't the water that was dangerous; it was what had happened *in* the water that had caused the trouble. There were no sharks in Ireland.

His dad, who'd been so cautious and protective to start with, began to encourage him, saying he shouldn't wait too long. 'It's the same as getting back on a horse when you've fallen off.'

Jay didn't think it was the same.

He remembered Lonnie's instructions before they'd left. *Patrique, make sure he gets back into the water as soon as he can.* And the way Jay's dad replicated Lonnie's voice so well made Jay feel sad. He believed his dad missed Lonnie too, but they couldn't ring her or email her or FaceTime her – because of his dad's campaign to keep them cut off from most of the civilised world.

'We're going to spend our time making proper real-life, flesh-and-blood friends here in Cloncannor,' Dad kept insisting.

'Yeah, right, that's working out great for me,' Jay replied, thinking about how he'd wrecked his chances with Jess and how he wouldn't be friends with that other crowd of side-eyers if they were the last people left alive.

The rehabilitation pool was fine for a while, even fun, but after a few weeks it just felt like a bath: hot, uncomfortable, confined. He needed the sea. It was time to go back in the water. The first thing to do was to start with a simple swim. Everything else would follow.

It took a long time to get his wetsuit on. He peeled

it carefully over the still-tender places. It didn't exactly hurt his scar, but he could feel the suit pressing down on it. He stretched his arms up to the sky like a morning worship and did ten squats. And he felt his injured side throb and pulse a little, but there was something else too – an agile strength, like a secret that had been returning to him all this time, rising from deep inside, shifting, straightening.

He and his dad walked together from the cottage to the beach and for a second Jay felt another old feeling: that he was his dad's miracle, his gift.

His dad took binoculars from his bag and began twisting the lenses. 'I'll be keeping a close eye, watching you every second, right?' he said. And Jay ran, unswerving and fast, away from his dad, towards the water.

If Jay faltered, it was one of those invisible hesitations that no one else would have spotted. Wading in, electric jolts of cold shot through him. He might have turned back, but he could feel his father's eyes on him, peering through the binoculars, rigid and watchful.

It was this mixture – his dad's surveillance, the tightness of his wetsuit, the coldness of the water – that made a kind of rage ripple through him, a vicious urge to split the stain of this ocean wide open. Almost in a single movement, he lunged forward and then he plunged down. An icy salt-sting loosened a silence-stiffened knot inside him.

This was a new kind of shock. It was as if he'd broken some dark spell that had been keeping him suspended inside a cloudy cage.

Still watching anxiously from the shore, his father seemed to sense it too and began to shout. 'Well done, Jay! Look at you go!'

Jay couldn't remember how long he'd stayed in the sea with his father jumping and cheering on the sand. All he remembered was the feeling that this had been the most important swim of his life – like he was wrestling some old enemy he could not name. Stroke after stroke and kick after kick he could feel it: the beginning of something. Healing his wound. Settling a score. He'd gritted his teeth and swum with certainty, breaking through the surface like a seal, bellowing with anger he did not fully understand (because how could he be angry with the deep?) and with a victory that he did (because he was doing it. He was in the water swimming as well and fast as he'd ever done.) And there was no pain. And he was not afraid.

Later, warming up by the stove, Jay's dad put his hand on his shoulder and told him how proud he was, and his face had a crumpling just-about-to-cry expression that Jay could not look at.

'Dad, it's great to be swimming again, but it's not enough. I feel like a kid with you watching me like I don't know what I'm doing.'

'That'll only be for a while. Just until you find your sea legs again.'

'I've found them. Did you not see me? I really have, and the surf out there is amazing, and I don't think I need to wait any longer.'

It was time, Jay said. Time for a surfboard.

'Really? Are you sure?'

Jay's will was strengthening. He asked his father what the actual *point* was of going to the trouble to be near the sea again if he wasn't able to surf in it. 'That's the whole reason there is sea.'

The following day they headed to the Grangekellig surf shop. Jay lifted a blue and white Wavestorm out of the display and carried it to the till and they fitted it on top of the roof rack. And every so often on the way back to Cloncannor Jay opened the window and reached up to touch the board's smooth, curved edge until his dad told him to stop. And for the whole night he hoped for decent surf and kept his bedroom window open, listening to the sound of the wild Atlantic and all its promise.

By six the next morning the tide was perfect. Jay checked the beach and then ran back to wriggle into his suit and wake his dad, and race again along the grassy path and down through the dunes with his shining board under his arm. The waves' swishes and sighs beat out a rhythm on the beach, hitting the sand, sending shudders up through his body. And there was an old familiar excitement pushing him forward and none of the fear holding him back.

His dad was groggy and yawning and still in his pyjamas, holding binoculars in front of him as if they were a torch, stumbling behind, shouting, 'Wait, wait. Don't start till I'm there.' He hurried to take his place like a guard or a soldier on the misty beach.

Jay pressed his stomach to the board and felt again the shock of cold water seeping under his suit, on to his skin and pooling along the creases of his body and over his scar. He pulled his arms numbly through the water, making his way towards the foaming curves of green, wondering how he could have waited this long. Every few strokes he'd glance back at the clear outline of his dad's figure.

He dragged himself towards the foam. And his stroke was clean and he was getting closer and closer, and there was this excellent shiver on the surface of the water and soon he reached them: those rolling, toppling, growling waves. They were magnificent.

His scar seemed to twitch and tighten as he felt his skills returning and his courage coming back, toughening his muscles, steadying his heart, tensing his fists and giving him the speed that he thought had been lost for ever. To think how close he had been to the water this whole time. How easy it was to pull himself towards the surf and how rapid and unwavering he was, and how quickly he now set his sights on what he'd wanted all this time.

There was focus in him as he took the measure of the wave, lined himself up and waited. Before the moment came, he glanced at the shore and saw that someone else was there standing beside his father, and, whoever it was, he was glad there was going to be another witness to the spectacular thing he was about to do.

He felt the great surge of the water as he scaled it, and, as the wave lifted him, hidden pockets of darkness seemed to wash away and his nightmares unravelled, and his sadness for the things he had lost seemed to loosen its grip. He pressed himself up on to the board, raising his belly, sliding on to his feet, crouching, and then he stood.

This wave belonged to him, and it felt as if he had conquered everything, and in that instant it was the only thing that mattered. Moments like those are rare and fleeting, and Jay knew to soak it up, to drink in all its magic pieces: the salty air, the ocean-chilled wind, the foamy spray, the great curl above him, the rumbling whoosh beneath.

CHAPTER 14

JESS

Since Esme's ban every day had stretched out in front of me like one great big yawn. But there was something about this Sunday that made it seem different from the start.

Six thirty in the morning. I'd given up on the hope of sleep, so I rolled out of bed, threw on my dressing gown and pulled open the window to check the state of the surf. I could see it was perfect – sudsy curves and the lovely rounded shape of them. I didn't notice anything else at first, and then, when I did, I didn't know what I was seeing – a shape, barely more than a smudge, but then the shape simplified into someone at the waterline with a board under their arm. It was way too early for lessons, and this was the north bay. For a bleary, disorientated second I thought it might be Charlie, trying his luck on the wilder side of the beach, but then I remembered with a pang that he wasn't even in the country. The early morning light was thin and watery. A mist was clearing off the sand. I pulled the window to its full openness. The figure grew sharper.

The surfer stood for a moment between the sand and the sea.

I knew who this was then. It was Jay. Jay Danagher, paddling towards the breakers now – and a hundred different things began to dawn on me.

I scrambled into leggings, flung on a top, slid on my slides, tiptoed downstairs, slipped out of the back door and ran for the north bay.

I kept my eyes fixed on him the whole time, jogging along, barely able to breathe, and bumped right into his dad, which, of course, was the worst possible thing. Since the party Jay's dad had hated me too and wanted nothing to do with me, and if I ever wanted to change this, I'd have to give him a big speech. But I'd been avoiding that, and I'd nothing prepared and was no use when it came to impromptu off-the-cuff apologies that I hadn't rehearsed at least ten times in advance. Plus, it's a difficult thing to find the words to say sorry for your entire personality.

Jay's dad was looking out through a massive pair

of binoculars, and when he finally saw me he glared in a way that made me know for definite there were bridges to mend.

'Oh, Mr Danagher, hello. Isn't this great? I couldn't believe it when I saw him, and I had to get down here for a proper look, and I didn't know!' I blurted.

'Didn't know what?' he asked, unsmiling.

'That your son is a surfer!'

'Yes, yes, he is, We told your father when he called. Surfing is one of the main reasons we're here.'

'Oh, typical. Honestly, my dad never tells me anything.'

'Right, well, if you'll excuse me, I need to focus,' was his stern reply. 'He's a good surfer but he's never been in this bay before, so if you don't mind, I must keep a close eye on him . . .'

I sat down on the sand. 'Oh god, Mr Danagher, look, I'm really sorry. I know you're mad at me and you have a right to be, but I wish you weren't.'

'I'm not.'

'But you are, and I don't blame you one bit. I acted so badly at the party, all obnoxious, asking stupid questions and bombarding Jay, and taking his scarf. It was awful of me. I've been wanting to apologise ever since; it's just I haven't had the nerve.'

He glanced at me for a moment and then back to the binoculars, but something in him seemed a little less tense, less severe, and for a while he said nothing and we both watched Jay, making his way out to the waves.

'It was my fault,' he replied then. 'I should have explained more carefully. It's only natural to be curious. Anyone would be. I should have told you: Jay can't talk about his past. I hope you understand. He needs to move forward. And now, look at him, he is!' He handed me the binoculars and I took them and looked.

Jay rose on his board and sliced and twisted and sped on the Cloncannor surface of our ocean in a way I'd never seen – not in Esme, not in Charlie. No one had done what he could do. I couldn't look away. It was like music and there was joy in the shape of him and when I looked again at his dad, there were tears falling down his cheeks. And this was perfect, because me and Jay's dad were connected to each other now, the same way people are when they watch the sunrise together or go out in a thunderstorm.

But Patrick flicked away his own tears with the flat of his hand. I couldn't think of anything to say, and was glad I said nothing, because whatever I did say would definitely have been the wrong thing.

I was thrilled to see Davy arriving and running round the two of us in a blurry circle. Jay's dad patted Davy.

A million things were going on inside my head. Charlie was gone and Esme would never take me out on the ocean and my summer had been shaping up like a prison sentence, but now – everything could be different.

Jay was the strong surfer who could take Esme's place. Dad had promised. Jay had been sent to me. It was the only explanation. This boy, possessed of skills so natural that he hadn't even needed to mention them. I'd heard stories about people like this and their gifts of synchronicity. He was like a dolphin or a seal, more at home in water than on land, leaping and curving and swerving as if he would never stop.

'Good, isn't he?'

I hugged Jay's startled father then. 'Good? He's not good. He's amazing. He's magnificent. He's incredible.'

I texted my parents and Esme. Told them to come immediately to the north bay. Everyone stood on the north bend of the beach, shading their eyes and seeing for themselves how strong and skilled Jay was, and I knew Esme was raging inside but she had to give in because Dad had promised and it was official. One after the other, Mam and then Dad and then Esme shook hands with Jay and his dad, and that was it. From tomorrow I was going to surf with Jay. He was going to teach me. His dad would be the lifeguard in case of any problems. The summer plan was on again. I was going to be a surfer. It's actually incredible the way one single moment can turn a ruined year in a completely different direction.

Jay and I chatted for the rest of that day. I explained to him how much I hated myself for the way I'd been at the party.

'I can never strike the right tone. I've no instinct for getting to know new people. It's my parents' fault for making us live in a tiny town where nobody comes and nobody goes, except for the tourists, and they don't count. You and your dad are the only two proper newcomers I've ever met. I got carried away. So, like, sorry for being so weird that night. You'd barely been here a day, and I managed to mess it up.'

But then Jay explained that he hadn't thought there'd been a single thing wrong with me. He'd liked talking to me, he said, and he'd wanted to stay. It was his dad who had decided to exit stage left just as the conversation was getting interesting.

He said he was the one who should apologise to me. It was a stupid rule as far as he was concerned, and he'd much prefer to have been able to tell me what happened and how he'd got his scar.

'You don't have to. I understand. I'm not going to ask any more.'

But he said I deserved more than rude silence and a sudden hurried disappearance.

'It was an accident in the sea last year, in France. I got hurt. It took me a long time to recover. And my father's been sort of jumpy about me since then.'

'You're not serious!'

'Don't you believe me?'

'Of course I believe you. Why wouldn't I believe you? I'm just amazed at the coincidence. Blown away about how much you and me have in common.'

'What do you mean?'

'It's the same for me, the exact same!'

I told him how my parents and my siblings were also incredibly anxious about me being in the sea, and that the reason they'd spent my life conspiring to keep me away from it was because I fell in when I was a baby.

'It was no big deal but they never got over the thought I might drown or something.'

'OK, interesting, and glad it turned out OK,' he said, 'but that's actually nothing like what happened to me.'

I wanted to ask him what he meant but there was a look on his face that made me know it was time to drop the subject, and anyway we had to plan my first surfing session, which, if the weather held, was going to be early the next day. Me and Jay Danagher, surfing in Cloncannor bay.

'Make sure you tell me if I do anything annoying or strange.'

He said he would.

'Nothing interesting ever happens here, you see. You, Jay. You are the most interesting thing that's happened to this town.'

CHAPTER 15

JAY

'Am I?' Jay asked. 'Really?'

'You are. You totally are,' said Jess.

There was much more he wished he could say then but the moment had passed. Maybe it was too late. Perhaps it always would be. Another part of him felt it didn't matter now. They were going surfing together in the morning. Later, in bed, before falling into a dreamless sleep, Jay thought about how life can flip and twist just as quickly as a surfboard.

He woke thinking someone was screaming. It was seagulls. There was an unusual glow coming from outside and something smelled warm and still. It was one of those days. They happen all the time in

France, but in Ireland they are the rarest of things: still, hot, blue, cloudless, windless, clear.

He wandered down to the beach. Everything looked different in this kind of light. Jess was there already with her surfboard and a face like tragedy.

'No surf,' she said, throwing down her board. 'Not a ripple.'

She started pacing on the sand, furious with the beautiful sun and the glossy sea.

It was Jay's dad who suggested they paddle anyway; in the absence of surf this was the next best thing. At least it would be something to do. At least they could be in the sea.

Next thing, Jess's mother had arrived with a massive bottle of sunscreen and a cooler bag full of water and lots of hot-weather instructions. Jay felt a flicker of sorrow and a small swell of mother-envy in his chest but he let it pass. Jay's dad promised he would keep watch, showing Annie Flanagan the binoculars, which reassured her greatly.

'The water's almost warm!' Jess said, amazed.

They paddled out, the two of them like knives cutting into silk, leaving the sounds of the land behind. They lay on their bellies and drew their hands through the water, and Jess told Jay how astonishing he'd been on the surf the day before.

And Jay told Jess how weird it was to think that yesterday in this actual spot on the bay, the water was roiling and high, and how now it was flat as a mirror.

'That's the trouble with a beautiful day,' said Jess. 'What's the point in all this sun and clearness and loveliness when there's no surf? Also, give it another couple of hours and the whole country will be here. Noisy families and competing radios and picnickers and millions of other people invading our beach like it belongs to them.'

But right now it was still silent and clean in the freshness of the early morning and Jess closed her eyes. The gulls had quietened down and the echoes of indistinct voices drifted from the headland. Jay watched two terns zigzagging across the sky and diving into the water, piercing the surface like darts. And then somewhere, not far from them, was a very quiet sound of another presence in the water and a terrible fear grabbed hold of Jay.

Jay trembled and gripped his board. A great ripple was spreading out in widening circles round them. He looked at Jess who opened her eyes. Jay pointed.

'What?' Jess said. 'What?'

A small shape, making its own arrowhead of satin

waves, was coming straight for them, very fast, very definite.

Jay was holding on to Jess's board too, and grabbing on to her arm and repeating, 'This can't happen. I'm not going to let it. Be still, Jess. I'm responsible for you now, and I'll do my best. I'm going to try to get us to shore. Stay calm. Hold on to my board. I'll try to save us.'

He may have wanted to sound brave and strong, and he might have for a second, if his words hadn't been followed immediately by a staccato of frightened sobs.

'Jay, what is it? What's wrong?'

And Jay said, 'Jess, it's coming towards us. Look. It's a . . . it's—'

'JAY!' shouted Jess now, half alarmed at him and half laughing. 'What's the panic attack for? He always does this when people are out here.'

'Who always does?' Jay said, white-faced.

'Davy! It's only Davy!'

She helped an excited Davy up on to her board where he shook himself, spraying thousands of little drops of rainbowed water over them both.

Jay covered his face with his hands. Huge shudders shook his body.

'Hey, Jay, what the—Are you OK? What is it?'

'I feel like an idiot. I'm sorry.'

'There's nothing to be sorry about,' Jess said. 'Look. Look at us here, totally safe. Too safe if you ask me.'

They drifted in soft silence on the flatness of the water. Jess touched Jay on the arm. 'I think I need to know what just happened.' There was no unkindness in her words. It was typical Jess: all directness and honesty. 'What made you so scared? It doesn't make sense. You have to explain.'

He sniffed. 'Do I?'

'Yes. Because we're friends now, and that's what friends do. They tell each other the things they're afraid of. It's part of the friendship deal.'

And so it was out on the flat water that hot morning that Jay told Jess what had happened at Dellabelle Cove – the snorkelling and the earphones and the shark and the attack and his mother and her fearless death. He cried quietly, and Jess kept holding on to his board so he wouldn't float away.

She sat for a long time. 'Is it OK if I ask you some other questions now?' she said eventually, and Jay said she could if she liked.

'Is your heart broken over your mam?'

Yes, he said, but more for her than for him. He explained how he'd never known her and couldn't exactly miss her, but that he felt terrible that her life had been robbed because of him and the shark.

'Are you still in pain?'

He said he sometimes was, but it was much better. It had been very bad at first.

'Wow. What's it like to be attacked by a shark?'

He said he didn't actually know, explaining that he could only remember foggy bits of what had happened and nothing about the shark itself.

'That's awful,' she said.

'I know. It's the part that drives me mad. I thought the fear was gone, but today it came back. I hate the way it does that – from nowhere, rising up at me again randomly and unexpectedly. It's always a horrible surprise.'

'*I'm* not surprised,' she said. 'Of course you still get scared, and of course your brain has blocked things out.' What he was probably experiencing, Jess explained, was something like a blank-out. Esme and Charlie had told her about them. 'It's when people get thrown off their boards in the middle of a wave and they have this weird tangled-up moment where everything smushes together.'

'Yeah, that's quite like how this feels,' he agreed.

'Maybe if you try to remember before the

attack – what it felt like when you woke up that day, what you had for breakfast and stuff, and how you got to the snorkelling spot and everything, maybe if you go over those bits, it might jog your brain into remembering the rest?'

'Maybe.' But he could hear the flatness of doubt in his own voice.

'Just because you can't remember now, doesn't mean you've forgotten it for ever.'

'I have a terrible scar,' he said with a tremble in his throat.

'Of course you do. You survived a shark attack.'

Jay touched the visible part of it at the neck of his wetsuit.

'You can't be ashamed of it, or at least you shouldn't be. You need to know the story of your body.'

Jay said nothing but he was thankful. He didn't want to be careful about hiding himself any more, especially not in front of Jess.

Warm as it was, Davy had started to shiver and Jess reckoned they'd better take him back. Plus, Jay's dad hadn't specified a time limit, but by then they'd been out there for ages. They began their slow paddle back to shore.

'The reason Dad took me away from the party is

he never wants anyone to be told. It's top secret. He says I need to work hard to keep it out of my head.' Jay paddled slowly beside Jess, and Davy adopted an intense rigid pose, like he was listening carefully too. When they reached the sand, they stood in the paleness of the shallow water and lifted their boards and carried them under their arms.

'Anyway, I'm really glad I've told you.'

'Are you?'

'Yeah, because you're so great and because I've been wanting to tell you since you first asked. I know I can trust you not to tell anyone else.'

'If wild horses were pulling me apart, they wouldn't drag it out of me,' Jess said.

Jay smiled and the sun was still dazzling and the sand was still golden.

Jay's dad must have assumed what he'd heard was laughter, not fear. He suspected nothing about the conversation the two of them had had on the water. When they slid up on to the beach again, he was reading a newspaper.

'How was it?' was all he asked.

They told him it was brilliant.

*

That night Jay dreamed that he saw his mother struggling on the surface of the splashing water, and of his dad with his arms high in the air, running towards him, making strange noises. Trying to warn him, he guessed, about the shark.

He woke up trembling and covered in sweat, shaking his head from side to side the way a shark does with prey clamped in its pitiless jaws. It took a while to soothe his clattering heart.

'My mother gave up her life to save me. I am alive because my mother is dead,' he whispered. In a strange way, saying it calmed him as long as he didn't pay attention to the deeper part of him – the pit of guilt and despair.

Jess had asked for the truth and he had given it to her. You can't be expected to keep a thing like that to yourself. You have to tell someone.

If he went over the build-up to the attack inside his head, he might end up remembering what he had forgotten. Like jump-starting an engine, Jess said.

'Just before you go to sleep every night, take yourself back to that day,' she'd advised. 'Go over what you can remember, and then maybe what you can't will slowly begin to appear, like colouring in a picture, you know? You're safe now, Jay. I know it's a terrible thing that happened, but you're not in danger any more. Cloncannor is the safest place on earth. Your memories can't hurt you. At least, I don't think they can.'

Those words seemed wise and true to Jay, and they worked their way around him and they gave him courage. That evening he stood in front of the mirror, staring at his own body, following the wide line of damage from his neck and down his side. And not for the first time he traced his hand along the numb, scarred ribbon, feeling its ridges and bumps. His body was strong again, but the scar would always be there. And Jess's words echoed inside him: *You can't be ashamed of a scar. You need to know the story of your body.*

In the days that followed he tried, harder than he ever had, to remember.

He remembered the misleadingly happy alarm clock beeping early on the morning that felt so long ago now – full of the sound of excitement, just like he had been. He tried to pull himself back to the narrow, dusty road in France and to his dad's jeep, and to the hope that had been burning that morning in the hot light of the French shore. His new earphones had poured music into his head.

In the jeep that day he could hear the echo of his younger voice, talking to his dad.

'How old was I when I last saw her?' he'd asked.

'Six months.'

And Jay had said, 'Oh, right.' And he remembered that he'd thought about what a long time it had been since his mother had seen him.

He remembered how they'd reached the wobbly road that threw flat red dust up behind them like chilli flakes. She was going to meet them at the cove to celebrate. And he was going to show her what he'd learned to do since he'd last seen her: walking, for example, and talking and swimming and snorkelling. He'd wanted to take his surfboard too but his dad had drawn the line at that and, besides, there had been no surf that day.

'We're like a travelling circus as it is!' he remembered him saying.

The day had been clean and blank like a fresh white page. That magic feeling that often goes with early mornings – the feeling that this was a secret that no one else knew.

Dellabelle Cove was a secret kind of place. It would be hours before anyone else came to interrupt their privacy. He'd thought how clever his mother had been to plan it that way. She wanted it so that when she came, there would be no distractions, no one else to drag their attention away from each other or from the things they wanted to say.

Dad said she had her own reasons for leaving them long ago, but since he'd never told Jay what those reasons actually were, Jay was hopeful this would be the day he'd find out. He'd practised in the mirror. 'Em, Mum, Maman, why, like, as a matter of interest, why did you leave us when I was only a baby?' He'd tried to make his voice indifferent but there was no way of asking that question without sounding a bit weird. He hoped she'd maybe raise the subject without him having to ask. That would be the best thing.

'What do you think I should say to her?' he'd wondered, as they rumbled along the rocky cliff road and down towards the cove.

'Anything you like, mate,' his dad had said.

A few other questions had formed inside his head and he'd practised them under his breath too, low enough so his dad wouldn't hear. But, of course, in the end, none of them got answered. Those questions got buried that day in a deep, wet, quiet place, the same way the dead are buried in the ground.

He remembered that red cloud of dust and the jeep turning into the car park, and the croak of the handbrake and the roll of the sliding door opening, and them dragging the gear out and picking their way down the steep wooden steps and the blue-diamond glitter of the ocean.

They'd arrived ahead of her. *It's OK, that's the way it's supposed to be*, Jay told himself. But still he kept looking around for her.

'Listen, Jay,' his dad had said as Jay pulled on the snorkelling gear and adjusted his earphones. 'Look, it's hard for me to say this, and I probably don't need to. It's just I . . . I don't want you to feel too much hope. I'm sure she'll be here any minute, but it's worth keeping in mind that your mum is not like other people.'

'What do you mean?' Jay had asked.

'I mean, don't get your hopes too solid. Your mother's the kind of person who sometimes says she's going to do something but she doesn't always follow through.'

The words 'mum' and 'mother' always seemed strange to Jay when they came from his father's mouth, as if they were words neither of them fully understood. But this time Jay had known his dad was wrong. His mum had written to him. He'd read the letter about seventeen times. In it she said she had a really cool surprise planned but she couldn't tell Jay what it was and she told him not to mention anything about it to his dad. He was going to have to wait till they met on the beach, and it had to be really early in the morning so the surprise would have its greatest effect.

'Where is she, Dad?' Jay had kept asking.

'Jay, mate, whether she shows or not, we're going to have a brilliant morning, right?'

Jay hadn't been able to let that in. He knew she was going to show, but it was going to drive him crazy if he had to sit around stretching his neck and squinting up at the steps trying to see if he could spot her. That was when he decided he wanted to be in the water, swimming, so that when she came, this was what she would see: Jay and his strong legs and his surfer's arms, gliding though the water like a fish.

'Hey, Jay, if she doesn't come, it mightn't matter so very much, eh?'

Jay then put his earphones on and turned them up loud so his dad had to shout.

'You matter,' Jay's dad roared after him. 'Your life matters. I am paying attention to you, even if she doesn't come today. I'm cherishing your life every single moment!'

'OK, thanks,' Jay yelled back, and then sat at the edge of the water, positioned his snorkel and waded in with those huge stupid flipper steps – it would be just his luck if she arrived to see him doing that. He glanced up very quickly, but still she wasn't there.

He would not waste any more time. He remembered the gritty slaps of his flippered feet on the sand, and he remembered the way his breathing had been magnified inside his snorkel and turning up his waterproof earphones even louder and jumping into the water and swimming quickly, seal-like, towards the deeper side of the cove.

He'd shouted at his dad because suddenly it had occurred to him that he didn't want *him* to be waiting either, and whatever surprise his mother had planned, the *two* of them should be having a blast together, and in that way they'd be in control of the morning.

He remembered looking back at the shore and pointing at his father and, over the music, shouting, 'Come in, Dad!' and then seeing his father wading in with his clothes on and his father shouting something. Jay realised that must have been the moment his dad had seen the shark. Then there was a thunderous noise and the shape of his dad's body changed into something crooked and alarmed. Jay hadn't had time to turn around. And there was this massive bang, and then he could remember everything going black and blurry, and again just those scraps

167

were left: the quaking of the water and the foam a horrible dark pink, and a huge dragging, gaping feeling at the side of his body and weakness coming over him. He remembered how he could not hold himself up and that his eyes began to close, and he couldn't kick his legs, and he began sinking down, and just before this, when he brought himself back to that memory, he was always able to hear her: the voice of his mother shouting his name.

There were many details he still wanted to know and never would. Where had his mother been when she saw the shark? How come she was the first to get to him? And how could he ever disentangle the confusion that wrapped around him like black strands of seaweed, sometimes threatening to pull him under?

But it would be a waste to stay overwhelmed with grief and guilt, and it would be much better if he celebrated his survival and channelled her courage by not being afraid and by remembering every day that life is a miracle. That way she wouldn't have died for no reason. Doing his best to face down his fears and regain his courage – that would be the best way to thank her for the gift she had given him.

Someone had found his bright yellow flippers.

Apparently they had been Jay's disastrous mistake, his dad had explained in the hospital later on. Bright colours are like magnets for passing sharks. It's the reason serious surfers and swimmers wear black. But how was he to know that? No one had ever told him he needed to be wary of sharks. No one had ever mentioned there'd been any shark-sightings at Dellabelle Cove. Maybe those waters had always been shark-infested, but there'd been a big cover-up. If so, now he and his dad were colluders. If he'd known they were a hazard, he'd have taken the proper precautions. He worried about other kids who might meet the same fate as he had or worse.

It wasn't just Jess's questions that triggered the sharpening of these memories. It was the rare sunshine that reminded him of his past and the stillness of the day. He preferred the cloud and the rain. Though the whole town constantly cursed the Irish weather, there were loads of reasons to like it. For one thing nobody thought it was weird to wear a wetsuit every day. And so he could cover that wide and jagged mark on his right side and no one except Jess need know what had happened to him on that other day at that different time in that faraway sea.

CHAPTER 16

JESS

I should have appreciated the sunshine more than I did. After only a few days the rain came back heavier than before. Everyone got into bad moods and there was no demand for surfing lessons. Jay and I kept on offering to help teach. It only took me a couple of weeks before I was every bit as good as Esme was. I'd say that drove her mad in a way. I felt slightly sorry for her. But I felt even sorrier for myself. Surf school business shrank to a trickle. Mam and Dad could never remember it being so slow.

It was around then that Jay seemed to grow brighter and became quicker to smile and even faster on his feet. It was Jay who came up with the plan to lure the tourists out for lessons in the rain. It was one of those simple, inspired ideas that made everyone wonder why nobody'd thought of it before. 'They're going to get wet anyway,' he said with a shrug. It was the first time in any of our lives that we realised our family business wasn't actually weather-dependent. All we had to do was convince everyone else.

It would be my job to update our website and our social media presence. Jay said he'd love to have helped with that, only he didn't have any technology at home and no Wi-Fi and no phone. I did it late at night when everyone else was in bed. I made up profile pages with recent pictures of Mam and the kids' class and Esme with her advanced group.

Myself and Jay, who'd finally convinced Esme we could handle a class of our own, were going to be in charge of the 'intermediates'. I redesigned our 'meet the team' page with a separate section for each of us. I used my favourite photo of Esme and Charlie where they're standing close together, exactly the same height, flanked by their surfboards, laughing. I included a full list of the prizes they'd won, the medals, the awards. There were no good photos of me, but I couldn't leave myself out, so I chose the least awful of them – a recent selfie in the rain, with the sea all choppy and promising-looking behind me. *Teacher*, I typed.

Beside Jay's name I put a link to a slow-motion movie I'd made of him doing an especially brilliant flip, where the sharpness of Jay's skill was clearer than ever. His feet seemed to suck the board up off the water like barnacles clamping to a rock. His moves were like a dance. A gulch of seawater lifted with him and his board. As he twisted in the air, a halo of drops sprayed around him like a fan.

I stayed up very late and by the time I was finished the website had been overhauled. The next day my whole family was delighted with me. Esme sent the link to Charlie who sent a thumbs-up sign back, which was more than we'd heard from him since he left. Mam forwarded me a photo I'd never seen. I hadn't known she'd taken it. I hadn't even known she'd been there on the beach, but she must have been watching us. It was of myself and Jay on top of the waves together. And Jay is being a wizard, of course. But me? OK, I have a weird frown of twisted concentration on my face, but I'm standing the right way, and my legs are bent and my arms are doing what they're supposed to and I'm on top of a wave and I haven't been thrown off and it looks as if I'm gliding confidently towards the shore. As I recall, I fell off that wave a couple of seconds later, but in that moment I'm killing it.

Between us we rebranded the whole business. We called it Rainsurf School. And, using Jay's language, our new tagline said: IF YOU'RE GOING TO GET WET, WHY NOT GO BIG?

Jay and I handed out flyers. *Rainsurfing makes you hardy and resilient!* the flyers explained. *Learn to surf here, be able to surf anywhere.*

On my phone I made some more videos for Instagram and flooded all the socials with them until they'd gone viral. Soon we couldn't keep up with the bookings.

The summer was shaping up again and the sound of rain on my window didn't make my heart drop like it used to. The sound woke me up and thrilled me and made me feel as if thousands of big brilliant new things were just about to happen.

I didn't know it then, but a new thing was already happening and it was a big thing, but it was the opposite of brilliant and it was on its way, bent on ruining the summer for good.

Jay, Davy and I were in town. We'd run out of coloured paper for the flyers and were in Rita's bookshop, stocking up, when we heard the arrival – and then saw it. The sound of expensive wheels and then four big jeeps, each the same pale dove-grey, an orange logo on the side saying CARMODY SURF ACADEMY and huge racks on the top and sides and a big multicoloured trailer packed with surfboards. Jay and I weren't able to do anything except stand limply outside the shop hugging a ream of paper each to our chests, watching the convoy as it passed.

That's when I saw the old gang was there, strolling out from behind the ice-cream truck, all with strange, thin, sly-looking smiles on their treacherous faces.

'Look what's coming to town!' It was Nick and he was grinning, and someone else might have thought it was a friendly, happy kind of expression, but if you looked at his eyes, you could see he was studying us quite carefully. Of course, I knew almost straight away that this spelled something bad for us. Flanagans' Rainsurf School was about to be blown out of the water. In the old days, when we used to be friends, Nick Carmody used to go on and on about how he had a load of cousins from Dublin – all surfer entrepreneurs, constantly on the lookout for new opportunities. I hadn't taken much notice of him then, had barely listened, not really believed him, and neither had anyone else, but now there they were in front of us. It turns out they weren't figments of Nick's boastful imagination but real people, a whole grown-up-looking gang of them, parking their fleet of jeeps beside each other on Main Street at selfish angles so anyone walking by would have to squeeze past or go out on the road. We watched five slim, tanned, smiling people leaping out of those sleek jeeps and unloading the boards, laughing away to each other like they were sharing an enormous complicated joke that nobody else would ever be able to understand.

And there were Bonnie and Ciara jumping around and giving high-fives to the new arrivals and glancing over at us every few seconds, subtle as thunder.

I said, 'Come on, let's get out of here. Let's not have them see us gaping at them.' We had our pride and our dignity to protect. But it was like our feet were nailed to the concrete of Cloncannor Main Street, near the chip van.

There was sizzle and smoke as Cian and Jimmy threw on baskets of chips, shouting to ask if anyone wanted any. But we couldn't answer because we were staring at the surfers and hearing the music that blasted out of the windows. The air smelled suddenly of coconut oil.

'Hey! Are you here for chips or what?' Cian said, not to me but to Jay.

'Come on, let's go,' I said again, but Jay said we shouldn't scurry away. We should stand our ground. Not look intimidated.

'Sure. OK, yeah, two,' he said.

Cian handed out scalding white bags stained with vinegar and sprinkled with salt. We stood there, cooling the fat chips between our teeth for a minute at a time. If you didn't do that, those chips would rip off the roof of your mouth.

In the end, Jimmy came out from behind the oil vats to peer at the developments.

'Will we tell you what's going on over there?' he shouted.

'New operation in town,' said Nick, and then Bonnie popped up and said, 'Surfing school on the north bay,' as if they were part of some flash mob. And then Ciara jumped in between us and whispered, 'Gonna blow you outta the water!' and they all crossed their arms and stood with their legs apart like a band of superheroes gone wrong.

I realised that Jay and I must have looked like total fools still gawking, vinegary chips slicking our fingers.

'You're right,' Jay said to me, ignoring the others. 'Let's not hang around.' He blinked a few times as if coming out of a trance and we hurried away, back to our part of the bay, where Esme was out on the deck waxing surfboards that suddenly looked shabby and battered. She was whistling a happy kind of tune and I wondered if I'd have the heart to tell her the news.

'What's up with the two of you?' she asked cheerfully.

There was no way of keeping the convoy a secret and anyway Jay beat me to it and told her before he had his chips finished, delivering the news through a muffled mouthful, spitting little pellets of chip flesh out into the air.

Esme put down the board and asked us if we wanted a cup of tea, a strange thing she sometimes did at moments she sensed were significant, even though in the whole time we'd known Jay, we'd never known him to drink tea.

'Esme, you should see their huge jeeps. They're massive. You should see the equipment,' Jay said, while I sat silently, too shocked to say anything. Jay explained about the music, and about how they were taking over the town, and setting up on the north bay in direct competition to us.

Esme did not look devastated. She looked a little bit interested, a little bit quizzical. She stared out over the sea, thinking, and then announced, 'Sure, look, a bit of competition can be a good thing. It'll keep us on our toes. Perhaps our current income stream might get a bit of a knock-back, but you never know.

178

There might easily be room for two surf schools. Since you and Jay rebranded us, we can barely keep up with the demand as it is. We might even be able to collaborate with them. Don't assume the worst-case scenario, guys. That's never a good idea.'

But the Carmodys were not benign competition. This was a hostile move and soon everyone knew it. Within a week almost all our surf students stopped coming, even the babies.

We were losing a battle we'd never asked to be part of, defeated in a war that we'd never wanted to fight.

Carmody tents and pergolas got erected on the beach at the beginning of every day and were not taken down until late at night. The Bannons moved their food truck and sold chips and burgers and milkshakes right there on the north bay, which blared with music and was clustered with people who could sign up online and then show up on the beach. When I passed on my way to call for Jay, the old crowd and the new Carmody cousins would whistle or jeer, or in some other way try to make me feel mortified and small.

I thought about the work my family had done and what my parents and Esme and Charlie had built, putting this place on the map, and how Jay and I were now part of that. They were taking it from under us.

They called themselves the Showerspray Surf Academy, which, as far as I was concerned, was basically plagiarism. Soon they had over fifty thousand followers on Instagram.

We passed the town hall every day, where Nick's mam started a surfers' salad bar, and one morning we saw Nick eating a bag of carrot sticks. He gave us a horrible smile and offered us a carrot the same way you'd offer someone a chip. No thanks, we said.

'We can't let them get away with this,' I said to the rest of my family. But Esme, Mam and Dad said there was nothing we could do and it was much the best thing if we didn't worry about it. I pointed out that in the history of people being told by other people not to worry about something, zero people have actually stopped.

The Carmodys had taken over the corner on the north bay, near Jay's own swimming spot and the jetty where he sometimes rinsed his suit or tied his board. There was nothing to be done. My anger sputtered and spat inside me like bacon on a frying pan.

CHAPTER 17

JAY

They still had the waves, Jay reminded her. No one could take them away. And without a teaching schedule they could be out in the water for as long as they wanted, doing the thing they liked best.

Jay's dad was busy with the stall during the days, and with his painting in the studio way into the night from where Jay could hear the sweep and scratch of brush and palette knife. The herby smell of cut grass became familiar to Jay. He always left his window open so he could hear the whisper and whoosh of the waves. There was a remoteness about his father as he went about his work or sat up on the drive-on mower, and Jay had the creeping realisation that there was some new, unnamed distance between them now. Something had happened to silence them in each other's company. They never spoke to each other in French any more.

Jess had only asked him once. But her question had reminded him of all the questions that still spun around inside him. *What's it like to be attacked by a shark?* He wished he knew. He wanted to remember.

One day, he and Jess sat at the end of the jetty, dangling their legs over the edge, hoping for some decent wind. Jay explained that he had some research to do, and asked her if he could borrow her phone. Jess handed it over without a word.

At last he googled 'Dellabelle Cove', but there was nothing about a shark attack. The confidentiality agreement must have been why there was no mention of it. Jess jumped down and started to paddle in the shallows while he stared at the screen, searching some more. There *was* an article about Dellabelle but it wasn't about a shark; it was about another awful accident. A boy, also thirteen, had been badly injured by a boat's propeller while in the water, almost killed, then helicoptered off the bay, just like he had been, and taken to the same hospital in Marseilles. They didn't give the boy's name but Jay recognised the doctor. Pierre Lambert! Dellabelle Cove must have been cursed. A shark attack *and* a boating accident.

He wondered about the other injured boy, and what his name might have been, and realised that he must have been in hospital at the same time; it was a pity it hadn't occurred to anyone to introduce them. And when he thought about it more, it puzzled him that no one had. Not Pierre or Tom or Marie-Bernard or Lonnie or Beatrice or Jacques had thought that he might have liked to talk to someone his own age, who'd been injured at the same cove. He was suddenly annoyed with them all, but thinking about them made him feel a kind of nostalgia for the hospital and for Pierre and Lonnie and all the team and how they'd been so kind to him. For the first time in a while he became sharply conscious of his scar under his clothes, and along that line a burning ripple moved through him.

He thought about his dad's crazy rush to leave everything behind. He worried that he hadn't said proper thank-yous to any of them. He thought about Louis and his friends at school and the club. Under his breath, he tried to speak some French sentences and words, but the language felt like an old song whose tune he could only half remember. As he watched Jess, who'd been joined by Davy, splashing down there in the Cloncannor water, a private, ineloquent sadness seeped through him.

'How's the research?' she shouted, shielding her eyes from the glare of the water.

'Fine. Do you need this?' He held up her phone and Jess shook her head.

'Knock yourself out. I'm in no hurry,' she replied.

And so he did some more googling

According to the Shark Trust website, sharks are not lurking underwater planning to devour you as soon as you go for a swim. They'd much prefer to stay out of the way of humans and they pretty much wish humans would do the same for them.

More than seventy-three million sharks are killed by humans every year, and every year about six humans are killed by sharks and most of those are probably just accidents. Sharks don't like the way humans taste. The largest of humans wouldn't be as fatty or juicy as a seal, for example, which has a layer of blubber that sharks find delicious.

He probably meant to take a small nibble, Jay thought, strangely comforted, before realising, *Mum might have died for no reason, because when he found out I was a scrawny human, he would have spat me out and sped away like a torpedo.*

Statistically there is a one-in-eleven-million chance of being attacked by a shark.

Jay was one in eleven million.

Just then, some new information appeared on the screen in front of Jay's face.

The shark that attacks you is the shark you do not hear.

'The shark that attacks you is the shark you do not hear?' he repeated.

'What?' said Jess, walking back towards him now with Davy wagging along beside her.

'Jess. *The shark that attacks you is the shark you do not hear.* Look!'

He showed her the screen with a shudder of understanding that Jess did not share. 'Here, thanks for the lend.' He handed the phone back to her and said he had to go.

'OK, but call over later! Mum's making pancakes for tea!' she shouted after him.

'Not sure if I can,' he shouted back.

'Well, how about a swim down here tomorrow, first thing?'

But Jay didn't answer; he just jumped off the jetty and sprinted up the beach and through the grassy border and towards the dunes in the direction of his house.

His dad had been out all day, buying new equipment for the studio and the garden. Jay hoped more than anything that he'd be home by now and ran fast and then faster along the curve of the bay to reach him. He wasn't in the mood to talk to anyone else, but the Carmodys were clambering across the dunes to set up all their surf academy gear, the whole pack of them. Soon they'd have lit their own fire and would be sprawled out like they owned the place.

Bonnie approached him. 'Jay, on your own today? Where's your girlfriend?'

'I don't have one,' he mumbled.

'Yes, of course you do. She's not here today blabbering her face off?'

'Look, I can't talk,' said Jay, but Bonnie wasn't having it. 'Come over,' she said. 'Hang out with us! We're fun!'

'I can't,' he said.

'Jay thinks he's too cool for us,' said Nick, who'd appeared from behind the sand tufts flanked by Jimmy and Cian.

'What?'

'I said you think you're too cool.'

'What do you mean by that?'

'You know, too up yourself to be sociable.'

'Why would I want to be sociable with you lot? When you're blowing up the Flanagans' Rainsurf School and always being lousy to Jess,' said Jay, feeling a blush of loyalty.

'See, she *is* your girlfriend!' crooned Bonnie.

Jess was something better than that. She was his friend, but he wasn't going to start explaining this to Bonnie Gillespie or Nick Carmody or Ciara Daly or the Bannons. He had something urgent to talk to his dad about and it couldn't wait.

But Bonnie wasn't giving up. 'Someone called to the food truck this morning. She was looking for directions to you and your dad's place.'

'Who?' asked Jay, twitching to get away.

'A woman. She looked like a model. Your mother, maybe?'

Jay stared for a second but ran off then, not saying anything else. Jimmy shouted something after him but he didn't hear what.

When he reached the path through the dunes, he saw his father in the field of vegetables, lit by a sudden burst of sun. He waved at him but his father didn't see, and so he hurried towards him, slipping every few steps in his rush. His dad was holding out a tray of onions and lettuces, a half-smile on his face.

'What do you think, buddy? Just picked them this minute.'

'Yeah, great. They look really good.'

'And where've you been? I was starting to worry.'

'I need to tell you something,' Jay said, louder than he'd meant.

His father put down the tray and pointed towards the door. They both went inside. Jay followed through the hall and into the kitchen, where they each pulled out a chair at the table and sat facing each other.

'Listen, I know we're not supposed to talk about it but there's something really important I need to tell you.'

'Right then, go for it,' his dad said, wiping his hands on a tea towel.

'The earphones! They weren't to blame! I'd never have heard the shark anyway! Because guess what?'

His dad pinched the bridge of his nose, squeezing his eyes shut. 'What, Jay, what? Why are you even talking about this? I thought we'd put it behind us.'

'I'm telling you because you have to stop feeling guilty about it. It's made you silent and secretive and it's driven this huge wedge between us, and I love you, Dad, and I hate the way you think what happened was your fault. I'm telling you now: you have to stop blaming yourself.'

Jay stood up, speaking with the authority of the newly informed. 'It's a well-established fact that the shark who attacks you is the shark you do not hear! Silent as the sunrise, they are. That's how they get their prey.'

'Why are you telling me this, Jay?'

'Don't you see? I wouldn't have heard him no matter what! The earphones didn't do it. I wouldn't have heard him anyway. IT WAS NEVER YOUR FAULT!'

Jay's dad leaned forward. He put his head in his hands. There were speckles of paint in his hair. 'Where are you even getting this stuff?' he mumbled.

'Research,' said Jay simply, 'on the Internet. I borrowed Jess's phone. I've just been looking stuff up.'

The old dark bat-wing shadow was back, and a small pulse throbbed at the side of his father's jaw. On his face there was a terrible trembling anger.

'What, Dad? I wanted you to know. I thought you'd be glad.'

Jay's dad's hands curled into knotted fists and his eyes turned the strange colour of rage. 'Why would I want to know anything about that day or that time? Haven't I said this enough? Didn't I say it from the start? You're not allowed. You are free in so many ways, but I do not permit access to the Internet. Can't you accept that? Can you get that into your head? The Internet's a cesspit.'

There was a snarl in his father's voice that frightened Jay. Something was going on. Something bigger than he understood.

'No, Dad,' Jay said. 'I'm not going to get that into my head. You can't ban me from having an interest in my own past. Just because you don't talk about it and just because you don't want me to, doesn't mean it didn't happen. You don't have a right to control me. If I want to find out about sharks, I'll find out about them. You might be my father but you're not in charge of what goes on inside my head.'

Jay's father was silent. Jay couldn't look at him any more and turned away. In the tension of this confused moment there was a knock, small and sharp.

'I'll get it,' said Jay roughly, glad of the excuse. Before he opened the door he caught a familiar smell. The nuttiness of frangipane. The sweetness of lavender.

At first Jay didn't recognise the woman standing there. She belonged to another world and it took a while to realise who it was. Lonnie. The last time he'd seen her was in the hospital, and she'd worn quiet shoes and had an ID lanyard around her neck. Now she was wearing leggings and a baggy T-shirt with a cartoon shamrock and a pint of Guinness on it.

'Jay, dear Jay, look at you, so strong now and so wonderful; it's good to see you,' she said in English, and he wasn't totally sure but it seemed like the glittering in her eyes might have been tears.

'Wow, oh my god, Lonnie. What are you doing here?'

Both Lonnie and Jay turned to Dad, who was standing in the hall now, biting his lip. 'There'll be plenty of time to explain,' he said gruffly. 'Lonnie, hello, you're early!' He hugged her then and looked down at her face very closely. 'I would have collected you from the airport! Here, can I help you with your things.'

'*Patrique*, haven't you told Jay?' She walked towards the stool in the hall to sit, her face reddening.

'Not yet.'

'You've explained nothing?'

'Let me help you with the luggage,' Jay's dad repeated.

'Forget the luggage – I have only a small bag. The rest is being shipped.'

'You're shipping your stuff over to Ireland?' Jay said, confused.

'Lonnie,' whispered his father, 'I'm going to

explain it gradually. I didn't want to land everything on him in one go. He has a lot going on, you see.'

Dad made these ridiculous googly eyes at him and Jay shuddered at the thought of what Lonnie's arrival might mean, and suddenly he did not want to know.

It might have been nice to see Lonnie again if someone wasn't making a massive fool out of him.

'I'm going to my room,' he said.

'We'll talk about everything later,' his dad shouted after him, and Jay said, 'Yeah, right, whatever, do what you like.'

Jay didn't come out for the rest of that day. He could hear the voices of the Carmody crew through his open window but he must have fallen asleep, because he woke in the dark to hear his father singing 'Rainy Night in Soho' at the top of his voice. It was 3 a.m. Jay could hear Lonnie trying to get his dad to keep it down, but he just kept going to the end of the song, and then he began again.

'Tomorrow you tell him everything,' she was saying. *'D'accord?'*

'D'accord, d'accord,' Jay's dad slurred, and there was the creaking of doors and silence. But Jay was awake now and got out of bed and went to the living room where the uncharacteristic singing had happened. There was an empty bottle of champagne on its side

by the stove. Small streams of light had begun to sneak through the closed curtains.

When he strolled into the kitchen the next morning, Lonnie was at the hob, making creamy scrambled eggs, and there was fresh orange juice in a giant jug in the centre of the table.

'Jess was here but we told her you were sleeping in,' said his dad.

Jay frowned. 'You should have woken me. We were going to go for an early swim.'

'There are things we need to tell you,' said Lonnie.

'Like what?' asked Jay.

'Sit down,' said Lonnie, 'have some juice, have some eggs.'

Jay did not sit down. 'Just tell me. Tell me what's going on, please.'

'I'm moving in,' said Lonnie, glancing at Dad.

'Where?' asked Jay.

'Here. Into this house,' said Dad.

'Yes,' said Lonnie, moving closer to Jay's dad, and then her arm was around him and his was around her.

Jay pressed his lips together and waited for more explanation.

'You see, Jay, your dad and I, well, you know . . .'

193

Jay didn't know, even though he was beginning to realise.

'*Patrique*, please, you must be the one to tell him.'

Jay's dad stared into his coffee and spoke very quietly. Jay leaned forward, trying to listen.

'OK then, well, the thing is, Lonnie's here. She's moving in and will live here with us, and she's going to . . . We're expecting . . .'

'Expecting what?' Jay said.

But there was silence.

'What? Freak weather? Rain from the east? WHAT?'

And right then, Lonnie turned and lifted the kitchen apron up over her head and bundled it together in her hand and Jay saw the arc of a new shape in her, and he stood staring at them both, stunned at what he finally understood.

'Is it true?' Jay asked, as Lonnie's eyes swam and flashed.

Jay's dad did the weird grin he sometimes did when Lonnie was around. 'Jay? Are you OK?'

'Why would I be OK?' said Jay. 'How could I be OK when you surprise-attack me with this? How come no one ever asked *me*? How come no one bothered to tell me before now?'

'There'll be a new baby!' his dad said, 'in eight weeks' time,' as if this was somehow the cure for everything. 'You'll be able to help out. You can take him for beach walks. Change nappies.'

'What are you even saying? I'm never going to change anyone's nappy, right? I can guarantee you that.'

'Aren't you even a little bit glad about this news?'

'No, I'm not.'

He slammed his door loud and kneeled on the floor and thought back to the hospital when Lonnie and Dad were getting to know each other. He was an idiot not to have seen it.

He had to talk to Jess. Before he left, he marched back into the kitchen. 'Can I just ask . . . I mean, can I check?'

Lonnie and his father looked at him, open-faced and receptive.

'Will this baby . . . is it, I mean, I presume it will be my sibling. Like, have I got that bit right?'

Lonnie and his father nodded.

'How did you stay in touch? How did you know?'

'Letters,' explained his dad.

'Right, and will this baby call you "Dad"?'

'Yes, this baby will, all going well.' Dad reached for Lonnie's hand and Jay looked away. 'And this will be the first time Lonnie will have someone calling her "Maman",' said Dad.

'You can call me "Maman" or "Mum" if you want to too. I'd be fine if you did.'

Jay looked into Lonnie's swimmy eyes. He did not feel the things she wanted him to feel.

'Why would I do that?' he seethed, taking a step back, any threads of tenderness falling away. 'I had a mother. Just because she's not here, doesn't mean she can be replaced.' He stared her down.

Lonnie's frown was a straight line of sorrow across her forehead. 'I didn't mean—I only thought, because, you know, because of the situation.'

'Lonnie –' Jay spat the words out like bullets – 'I'm not calling you "Maman" or "Mama" or "Mum" or anything like that, OK?'

'I'm sorry. I just thought it would be easier. Less confusing.'

Jay could see Lonnie looking to his dad for support but his father was taut and silent.

'Easier?' Jay laughed bitterly. 'Less confusing? What do you mean by that? Calling a random woman my mother? What's easy about that?'

Lonnie's hands were shaking.

'OK, Jay, that's quite enough,' said Dad, but Jay wasn't going to do what his dad said any more. He was going to decide for himself.

'Why would I call you my mother when you're not

my mother and you've never been my mother and you're never going to be?'

Lonnie was hugging herself and Jay could hear the deliberate breathing of the exercises she'd once taught him, and he watched her holding on to her bump as if it needed extra protection, as if there was danger nearby. 'I didn't mean to upset you,' she whispered.

'I'm not upset. I just don't really know why you'd want me to tell a lie for the rest of my life.'

'Jay! Knock it off, please,' said his father.

'Of course. I wasn't thinking,' she said, sitting now on the stool, which creaked under her weight. 'It was stupid of me. I should have been more sensitive. I should have known how much the whole thing must still affect you.'

The way she said 'the whole thing' was so unusual, the way she spoke those words, heavy like wet sand, the way she looked up at Jay, with that secret air that had sometimes hung over her and his dad when they were still in France. 'I don't care what you call me. It's only that I'd like to be able to talk to you.'

'There's nothing to talk about,' said Jay, heading through the front door and up the twisted path.

CHAPTER 18

JESS

I'd called to Jay early. We were supposed to be going for a swim. The woman was such a startling sight, her hair and her lovely skin and how sweetly she'd smiled at me when she answered the door. For a second I didn't think she was real. I introduced myself, but friendly as she seemed, she didn't introduce herself back, said Jay had some stuff to deal with at home and that she'd tell him I'd called and then she sent me away. There was something going on in the Danaghers' house. I was so curious about it I thought I might vomit.

When Jay called to my door and I saw his face of chaos I thought for a second something awful had happened.

'I have terrible news,' he said, out of breath.

'What?' I held on to the door frame, bracing myself.

'Dad has a girlfriend.'

'That woman? The woman in your house? She's Patrick's girlfriend?'

When he nodded, I let go and twirled around with the thrill of it. 'Oh my GOD! She's GORGEOUS! The whole town's going to go crazy! I thought you said the news was terrible!'

He frowned. 'She's moving in with us,' he explained grimly.

I clapped my hands together.

'Jess, stop. You don't understand. There's more.'

'Of course there is! Tell me everything!' I said, pulling him towards the kitchen.

Mam appeared, her hands and hair covered with flour. 'Jay, love, wonderful! Come on in. I'm making cherry scones.'

'Mam, we don't have time for scones,' I said, and Mam looked amazed because in the history of my whole life I've never not had time for scones. But that day I was feeling extremely grown-up and mysterious, and when you feel like that, your appetite disappears.

'Jay and I are going for a walk on the beach,' I announced.

'Don't be ridiculous – it's pouring,' exaggerated Mam.

'It's fine. We need the exercise.'

'OK, well, take coats,' she shouted as we headed down the path, not a coat between us.

You could hardly have even called it rain. It was the soft kind – more like a thin cloak of mist being laid gently on the land.

'Right, take it from the top. I want every single detail. This is so brilliant.'

'It's not brilliant. It's dreadful,' Jay replied, biting the nail of his middle finger.

I collected a few decent skimming stones and we wandered towards the grey table rock, climbing up. I threw a stone into the water and then handed him one, and he threw it, and then I threw another and we took turns like that for a while and I did my best to be patient and waited for him to explain in his own way.

He told me about how she'd shown up out of the blue. He told me that he hadn't a clue she and his dad were together, and he felt stupid that he hadn't twigged it. Jay put his hand to the scarred side of his neck, the nervous habit that I thought had disappeared.

'She's pregnant,' he said, and I was silent as the shiver of a fresh thrill danced inside me.

'Like, she and my dad. They're having a kid.'

'OH MY GOD!' I wanted to hug him right there, only he didn't look like he was in the mood.

'What's her name?' I asked.

'Lonnie,' he muttered.

'LONNIE!' I said. 'Lonnie what?'

'Lavelle,' he muttered again.

'Oh, even her name is splendid. Nothing could be more perfect! This is amazing. When's the baby due?'

'I don't remember.'

'Jay, you're useless! You need to find that out ASAP! Everyone's going to want to meet her. Mam and Esme will organise the baby shower. You know what they're like. Any excuse for a party.'

But Jay did not feel the things I was feeling or think the things I thought. He just stared at the sea.

'Where did they meet?'

Stricken with betrayal, he looked into my face.

'That's the worst of it. In hospital when I was barely conscious. She was my trauma recovery therapist. That's how they got to know each other.'

'They must've got to know each other very well.'

'Yeah, I know, right?' he said with a shudder. 'It's been arranged for months. He asked her to come ages ago, and she decided she would, and now she's here for good. My dad never told me anything, not until she rocked up.'

'But how did they keep in touch? Considering you've zero Wi-Fi and no phones.' I dangled my legs over the edge of Table Rock, thudding the stone face with my heels.

'The old-fashioned way, with letters and envelopes and paper and pen and stamps and post offices.'

'Oh my god, that is SO romantic.' I handed him another stone.

'It's not romantic. It's weird and strange,' he said, wrapping his fist around the stone like he was trying to squeeze blood out of it.

'But you're going to be a brother. You're going to have a sibling.'

'Yeah. Don't you think that's something a father would get round to telling his son?' His stone hit the water with a thwack.

'Maybe he wanted it to be a surprise?'

'Well, it's definitely that.'

'Your dad meets your therapist in hospital and they fall in love and she's having his baby. You couldn't actually make that up! It's the most glamorous thing I've ever heard!' I shifted on the rock and lay back and stretched out my arms.

'Stop, Jess.'

'WHY does that kind of stuff never happen to me? Why are my parents so BORING and ORDINARY? Why don't I get to have a love-child sibling from the south of France? You're so lucky.'

'Jess, shut up. Stop talking. Never say that again.'

'Why?'

'Because there's nothing good about this, and nothing glamorous about it, and I'm the opposite of lucky.'

'But everything about you. Your secrets, your scar, the shark that we're not allowed to talk about. I wish I was like you – silent and interesting. Everyone's OBSESSED with you.'

'No one's obsessed. You're the only person in the town who's any way decent to me. The rest of them are horrible.'

'What do you mean?'

'You know, that whole gang. The Bannons and Bonnie and Ciara and Nick, and the Carmody crew – the lot of them. What's worse is it's in my face these days, right there by the jetty. Every time I want to go for a swim there they are, whispering to each other quietly and laughing out loud as if I'm the butt of some joke or other. And they're nosy, and they already know Lonnie is here. Last night, Bonnie wanted to know if she was my mother.'

'What did you tell her?'

'I didn't say anything. I just walked away.'

'Good. Exactly right. In a way I'm glad they're being horrible.'

'Why?' asked Jay, squinting at the water.

'Well, it means our friendship is safe. Since you got here, I've been constantly worried that they'd turn you against me and lure you into their world and then you'd leave me on my own.'

'That will never happen,' said Jay with the certainty of someone who thinks they can predict the future.

'They used to be my closest, most important friends. And then I lost them because of this stupid thing I did, and it tormented me, and it still does. And I worry that the same thing will happen to us. Like, I'm not expecting you to feel sorry for me. You've faced much bigger problems in your life, but the thing is, Jay, I've had bad things to cope with too.'

'Everyone has bad things,' he said. He put his hand on my shoulder and it was as if he contained the heat of a golden sun.

Then we jumped off Table Rock and it didn't look like the Carmodys had set up yet so we decided we'd walk the whole of the north bay and over to the jetty. As we wandered, though, we saw a figure in the distance, slowly getting bigger.

'Oh, crap. I hope it's not one of them.'

But it was. Bonnie Gillespie.

'Found your girlfriend, again, I see,' she sneered at Jay as she passed us.

Jay couldn't take this. 'I've got to go,' he said to me, and he stomped off in the opposite direction. I couldn't blame him.

'Hello, Bonnie,' I said, hard and cold as ice.

Bonnie peeled open a pink square of bubble gum and popped it in her mouth.

'Just to let you know, you might think you're cool, and you and Nick's gang might have expensive brand-new gear, and the surf academy sounds very fancy, and you might be rubbing it in our faces and showing off right on Jay's doorstep, and your website might have animations and you might think you're all that, but you'll never be as good as Flanagans' Rainsurf School, and you know why?'

'Why?' said Bonnie, blowing a big pink bubble.

'Because you don't have Jay Danagher.'

Bonnie burst the bubble with her teeth and gave me one of her slow blinks. 'I don't know why you're boasting about him,' she smirked. 'Banging on as if there's something special about him. What's so great about him? I mean, OK, he might have a pool in his back garden but it's tiny. And there might be a gym in his house but that doesn't make him special either. Only narcissists have gyms in their houses.'

I could practically see a green mist of envy seeping out of her. That was the moment to walk away, just

206

like Jay had done. I should have left her there with her jealous thoughts.

Part of me knew I was about to do a terrible wrong, but I was caught up in something that felt bigger than me. I couldn't stop myself.

'He's not a narcissist. Jay Danagher is the total opposite of anything like that. For your information the pool's not supposed to be big. It's a treatment pool. It's for rehabilitation. So is his gym. He needs them because he's recovering.'

'From what?' asked Bonnie, her blink rate speeding up slightly.

I shouldn't have said it. I should have stayed calm and kept Jay's secrets to myself like I'd promised. I should have told her to mind her own business. But I could feel it coming like a wave, as if I had no choice.

'He's recovering from a SHARK BITE. Before he came to Ireland, Jay Danagher was attacked by a shark.'

Bonnie stopped chewing her gum. Her eyes flickered with a new kind of light.

'Yes, that's right, you heard me.' A strange thrill filled me. 'You should know what Jay Danagher is made of. Maybe you'll keep that in mind the next time you see him. Maybe you'll stop being so mean.'

'We're not mean,' she said, pretending to look hurt.

'I don't care about you being nasty to me any more – like, I'm used to that, and I probably deserve it, but Jay doesn't. He's literally done NOTHING to you, and he's recovering from this terrible thing and it's time you realised how brave he is, and it's pure lousy to think or talk badly about him.'

'But we haven't—'

'And plus, he's a better surfer than the whole gang of you put together and he isn't afraid of anything considering how he was practically ripped in two by the jaws of a huge shark and managed to escape.'

'Is that really true?'

'Yeah,' I said. 'Hundred per cent.'

'Where did it happen?'

'In France.'

'When?'

'Last year. And if everyone knew about it, none of them would be going anywhere near your stupid surf academy. They'd be queuing up to learn with us, to learn from Jay. And also, for your information, his mother died trying to rescue him, so, hey, Bonnie, another bit of advice for you, you shouldn't ask about people's mams unless you happen to know their mams are still alive. It's very tactless.'

'I . . . I'm . . . sorry,' she said, stumbling over her

words, and her lips wobbled and she lost her warrior stance.

'You think you're so great, but you're not, you know. People can come down here with shiny wheels and new surfboards or whatever they like. He's faced a monster of the sea that you couldn't even imagine.'

Shut up, Jess, I tried to instruct myself inside my head, but I was on a roll. 'Don't you EVER try to act like you're better than Jay.'

'So how come no one knows?' Bonnie asked, regaining her composure, her words coming out all leisurely again, full of some meaning that I did not understand. 'How come he and his dad have never mentioned a shark? I'd have thought the whole town would have that story by now.'

'Because it's a SECRET!' I shouted, loud enough, admittedly, for the whole town to hear. 'He doesn't want to draw any ATTENTION to himself! He's not a boaster. He doesn't feel like talking about it. It's a traumatic thing that happened, and he prefers to keep it to himself. What's so surprising about that? Why should he reveal the details of his life to people like you? He doesn't know you. He doesn't even like you. He's not going to go around telling you his life story.'

'Yeah, well, I don't get why it's a secret,' said Bonnie, looking at her nails before adding: 'You only make something like that a secret if it isn't actually true.'

'It is true. But wait, I know what's going on here. You're jealous. That's what it is.'

'Haha,' she chirped. 'I so am not.'

But it was obvious she so was. As I walked away from her, a new power rose in me, because Jay Danagher was my friend, not hers, and because I knew him really well by then and she didn't, and because her whole gang put together weren't anywhere near as fantastic as Jay was, and they never would be, and she knew it.

CHAPTER 19

JAY

When Jay got home the car was not there. Lonnie and his dad had gone out. *Probably to buy nappies and cots and baby clothes*, he thought. Still, he was glad because he didn't want to talk to them. By the time he heard the car pull up and the click of the lock, it was late, and Jay had gone to bed. His dad knocked on his door but he ignored it.

Jay barely slept, woke early, put on his dressing gown and followed the grassy path through the dunes, over the hill and down to the place that was already part of him.

Seagulls were swooping over the sea's speckled skin. Cormorants leapt from their basking spots, their necks curling, their sleek bodies diving under the water and then returning to the surface with silver wriggling prizes.

Jay looked up at the sky and down to the ground, figuring out how many days there were until he would be a legal adult. He found a black stick of driftwood and with it he scrawled calculations into the sand. Two thousand, one hundred and five. He used it again to calculate that this was fifty thousand, five hundred and twenty hours, which was three million, thirty-one thousand and two hundred minutes. Which was a hundred and eighty-one million, eight hundred and seventy-two thousand seconds. That's how long he'd have to wait. All those seconds standing between him and his escape. He'd go back to France and never talk to his father again. He'd find Louis and tell him he was sorry for being gone so long. They might be able to pick up where they'd left off. Maybe there'd still be time to make another new start.

It was later, when Jay had headed to the shops for milk and bread, that he happened to bump into all five of them. The Nick-Bonnie-Ciara-Cian-Jimmy crew. They were wearing black T-shirts with TEAM CARMODY in huge white letters. He did his best to stay out of their way; feeling their eyes falling on him, he had no interest in sticking around. He squeezed by them and out of Spar. That was when Nick shouted.

'There he goes! Shark Boy!'

A hot sting of shock raced through Jay's veins, and the sound of water rushed in his ears.

He turned around. 'What did you say?'

'I said there you go, Shark Boy.'

'Who told you?' he asked, too stunned to hide his horror and his alarm.

'Who do you think? Jess Flanagan, of course. She told Bonnie about how you were attacked by a shark and how you survived even though you got badly injured. She said it was a secret, but, bit of advice: if you didn't want anyone to know, you shouldn't have told Jess Flanagan. You can't trust her with a single thing. We've no idea why you two are even friends.'

A blurriness overtook Jay then. He dropped his bag and the milk landed hard, exploding and then collecting in a white puddle at his feet. He had to get away.

He sprinted to the beach and ran along the south bay, and jumped on to the sand, and raced along the curve of the north bay, and past the surf academy base to the jetty and sat on the end of it for a long time, trying to clear his head of its rushing thoughts.

*

He heard a gallop on the sand before he saw them: Jess and Davy coming towards him. He stood then and readied himself.

'There you are!' she panted. 'I was wondering where you'd got to.'

'Jess, stop,' he said. 'Leave me alone. Do not talk to me. Go away.'

'Oh my god, WHAT?' she said, her face in that awful second turning from brightness to shade.

'I met your old friends in town just now.'

'And?'

'You told them? You told them all the things I told you never to tell anyone?'

'Jay, I—'

'I thought I could trust you. I thought you were my friend.' When Jess took a step towards him, he took a step back.

'Please don't say that. You *can* trust me, Jay. Let me explain.' Jess kneeled down in the sand. Davy began to lick her face.

'There is no explanation,' said Jay in a whisper. 'How could you? And especially how could you have told them? I thought you hated them all.'

'I do, but it's because . . . they were . . . I mean . . . I wanted . . .' Jess was faltering and her voice became weak; it seemed she had no way of explaining. 'I'm so sorry,' she said, her voice a thin thread floating away from them.

'It's too late to be sorry. Don't you see, Jess? Sorry won't take it back. Sorry won't turn it into a secret again. The story will get out now, and that's the ONE THING MY DAD SAID WAS NOT TO HAPPEN.'

'I thought you hated your dad now.'

'I do, but that's not the point!' shouted Jay.

Davy began to run from where Jess was kneeling to the jetty where Jay was standing, and then back and forth again, as if trying to close the gap between them.

'OK, fine, but I still don't know why you have to keep it a secret.' Jess's face had turned pink. She stood and grabbed Davy by the collar as if he too had become unpredictable. 'I think your dad is wrong to have made you promise never to talk about it. That is *your* scar, and she was *your* mother and it was *your* fight for survival. He has no right to silence you. No one should be that afraid of the facts of their life. No one should be that afraid of the truth.'

'Please stop talking,' was all Jay could say. 'I asked you not to do something, and you did it. You knew how important it was, but you still did it.'

'I'm sorry. You're right. I was wrong.'

'OK, so what are you doing here?' Jay felt a cruel

thing clanging like steel underneath the worried hurt.

She lowered her eyes. 'The waves are so great, and they're getting better. I thought you'd come surfing with me. That's nearly always why I'm here.'

'I'm not going surfing,' he said.

'OK, well, look, maybe later?'

'I'm not going surfing with you now, or later or ever. I'm not surfing with you any more.'

'But what about Rainsurf and the lessons? We're winning some customers back again. Seven people are booked in for tomorrow.'

'I'm not doing that any more either.'

'What will I tell Mam and Dad and Esme?'

'Tell them whatever you like.'

'Jay, please, come on. I'm sorry. We can get over this. I can explain it properly . . . I think you're a hero. I wanted all the others to know what you've suffered, the courage you have. I wanted them to have some respect for you. I hated that they didn't. That's what it was.'

Tears filled up in her eyes and tumbled down her face, but there was no fixing what she'd done. Jay would not even look at her and there was nothing she could do but turn away, taking Davy with her.

Jay watched as Jess and Davy covered the curve of the bay, running, running, running, their footprints leaving a trail of shadows in the sand.

Jay spent a long time staring out at the water before he heard more footsteps approaching. He wrapped his fingers into tight fists and hissed, 'Jesus Christ, Jess. Go away. Leave me alone.'

But it wasn't Jess. It was Nick.

'Hey, wow,' said Nick, hands in his pockets. 'Like, sorry, but I'm here with an invitation. I was wondering if you'd consider joining the surf academy. We've already penetrated the market and we could do with someone with your skills.'

Jay glared at him. 'Maybe I haven't been clear, but if you were the last surf school on earth, I wouldn't join you. OK?'

Nick didn't flinch. 'OK, whatever you want,' he replied, digging his toes into the sand and making little holes.

Jay wished Nick would leave.

'So you were attacked by a shark. Wow,' he said, looking very intensely at Jay.

'I'm not going to talk about that. You're not even supposed to know.'

'Well, sorry to rain on your secret parade and everything, but we all know that's not true.'

'I don't care what you think,' said Jay.

'Listen, man,' said Nick, 'I don't know who you are, but there's lots that doesn't add up about you. You weren't really attacked by a shark. We've all googled it. The whole town has. There's no report or anything about it. What really happened was a boat crashed into you because you weren't looking. That's how you got your injury. But you didn't think that was a fancy enough story, so you made up a new one and you decided you'd prefer to be a shark-attack survivor and you only told Jess and you tried to make her keep it a secret because you knew everyone else wouldn't buy it. Little kids do stuff like that to big themselves up. It's OK. We understand.'

'That wasn't me,' Jay interrupted. 'That was a different boy. I was attacked by a shark but my father had to sign a confidentiality agreement. That's why it's not in the news, right? So shut up. Stop acting like you know everything.'

'But why would he have been asked to sign something like that?'

'It's the south of France – it relies on water safety and tourists.'

'Whatever you say, dude,' said Nick, walking

backwards away from Jay and then turning and sauntering off.

Jay thought about the many times he'd wanted to blurt out his secret to everyone he met. It had been hard work to keep it in. And now Jess had done it just like that. Telling a truth he hadn't been allowed to tell. He would never forgive her.

CHAPTER 20

JESS

J ay was never going to forgive me, I knew that, but
still I had to apologise. For three days, pretty
much non-stop, I tried my best. I called to the house.
There was no sign of Lonnie or Jay, only his dad. I
told Patrick that Jay wasn't talking to me, and his
dad said, 'That makes three of us,' as if this was
supposed to comfort me. Patrick told me it might
be better to give him some space on account of
there was a lot going on in his life right then, as if I
didn't know.

When cold-calling didn't work, I wrote 'Sorry' in
the sand near the path to his house, with the
Carmody gang watching and laughing at me. Not
that I cared. My dignity was gone by then and I only
wanted Jay back. I knew he'd see it. But he didn't
come and find me.

The next morning, I sent a note down with Davy, tied to his collar, but Davy came back covered in paint, and the note was still there, unopened.

I couldn't blame Jay. It was me who'd done something dreadful. I couldn't stop crying. I was never going to forgive myself either.

At home they kept asking what was wrong, but for someone who is famous for blurting everything out, I couldn't talk. I was sick with shame and regret. There was no time for such nonsense, Esme said. Our surf students were coming back and I needed to arrange the bookings.

The next day, I'd lots of emails to sort through on the info@rainsurfers.com account. One of the emails wasn't for me. It was for Jay.

Subject: Hello

I'm trying to get in touch with someone called Jay Danagher. I've been trying for a while now. I came across this website and saw his photo. Please can you ask him to get in touch? He doesn't know me, at least not very well, but I know him. My name is Elouisa Fougère. We were to be reunited last year but there was an accident. I am in Dublin for the next few days. I am his mother.

There was a hotel address and a mobile number but none of it actually made sense. I stared at the words for ages. I could hear the kettle boiling, and Dad humming a happy kind of hum in the kitchen and the sudden rain belting against the window like someone was out there, throwing gravel at the glass.

It might have been a crank, but it wasn't up to me to decide that. I had a responsibility to get the message to Jay. I printed it off and headed over to the cottage, fearing something that I did not understand.

'Go away, Jess,' said Jay again, this time on the doorstep of his cottage.

'I only came down because I have something.'

'I don't want anything from you.'

'I know but this is not from me. It's from someone else. Elouisa.'

He stiffened. 'What did you say?'

'"Elouisa." It's weird but you need to see it. She says she's your *mother.*'

He grabbed the paper from my hand so hard that it ripped in half. I dropped the torn piece on the ground and he snatched that too and there was so much confusion in him, and it wasn't just because of me any more. There was this look on his face. It gave me a sudden terrible feeling that I can't describe, like his burdens were so much greater than anything I had known.

He closed the door and I stood there stupidly, listening to the gulls who'd started screaming again.

CHAPTER 21

JAY

'What's that?'
'It's an email,' said Jay to his father, chilled with bitter shock. 'An email sent today. To the surf school. Jess printed it off to show me. Who, Dad? Who would you say is writing to me from France pretending to be my mother when you and I both know my mother is dead?'

The silence swelled like a bubble and then it popped.

'I never said she was dead,' Jay's dad said, low and shaky.

'What do you mean?'

'I didn't mean for you to believe it, but once you'd jumped to that conclusion I began to think it was for the best.'

Jay felt his legs becoming unsteady and he lowered

himself on to the stool in the hall. 'Sorry, what? For the best? You let me think my mother was dead, when actually SHE ISN'T? Maman isn't dead? Mum's alive?'

Dad said nothing.

Jay was trembling.

Lonnie appeared from the kitchen, and they both turned to her.

'Lonnie, is my mother still alive?'

Lonnie put her hand on the wall. 'Oh, *Patrique*,' she said first, shaking her head, and then: 'Yes, Jay. She is.'

'What happened, Dad? What really happened?'

Jay's father's face grew paler and he shook his head too, suddenly looking very lost.

Jay stared at him. The next thing he said was an accident, a single whispered word spoken in their old language: '*Pourquoi?*'

It startled them both. But if at that moment there had been the smallest chance of some kind of softness forming between them, Jay banished it and toughened himself. He steadied his body and strengthened his voice. 'Why? Why did you tell me this lie?'

And as his father began moving towards him, Jay already knew that the answer to this question was too big to explain.

'Stay away from me. I can't trust anything that comes out of your mouth. I don't even know who you are. Don't come near me.' He jumped up and backed away, like his father was a poisonous snake or a wild dog.

Jay focused on Davy, who'd appeared, his white curly coat multicoloured now, spattered with paint. The sight of him made Jay feel as if he might begin to cry. Davy had no idea how ridiculous he looked. Jay got the feeling he always got when he accidentally came across photos of pets dressed up in human jumpers or wearing hats. Sometimes people turn you into a ridiculous joke, and it's not your fault but you still get the blame. His father had done that to him. Made him the king of fools.

He stopped in the doorway and took a deep breath. 'The day we left France, Dad, and I wanted to talk to Louis and you took me to the club to see everyone and I couldn't believe how no one had come to say goodbye? No one came because you didn't tell anyone we were going, did you? You cut me off from my friends, Dad. Why did you do that? I loved those guys. I loved Louis most of all. They were like my brothers, and you took me away from them, and you took them away from me. And all those times you asked me whether

I remembered anything, and all those times you told me to stop trying to remember? That wasn't because you cared about me or wanted to protect me, was it? You weren't hoping that someday it would come back to me; you were praying that it never would.'

Lonnie put her hand on Jay's shoulder, but he shrugged it off.

'Don't touch me,' he said, and Lonnie's face of sadness didn't make him feel bad or awkward. He cared about nothing now. Nothing but the truth. Her chin was puckering, and he was almost sure she was going to cry too, but there's no instruction manual for when your ex-trauma-therapist-who-also-happens-to-be-your-father's-girlfriend-and-is-going-to-be-the-mother-of-your-sibling starts crying. This was uncharted territory.

'I can explain,' his dad said weakly.

'Don't bother.'

'What are you going to do?' his dad asked.

'It's none of your business,' Jay replied, grabbing his backpack and stuffing things into it. 'It's a terrible thing you've done, Dad.'

'I know,' said his dad, as Jay clattered through the front door, feeling nothing but the need to get away. Away from his father and the lies, and away from

Lonnie and the baby she was going to have, and away from the kitchen and the garden and the flimsy fences in this place that was supposed to be his home.

When Jay looked out at the sea, the horizon, normally sharp and clear, was quivering. There was a rancid taste in his mouth suddenly, like the metal ammonia of gone-off mussels. The taste of deceit. He spat on the ground.

Mattie Feeney's minibus lurched forward and Jay breathed out. He was glad to be leaving them all behind. He needed to see his mother. She was the only person who'd be able to make sense of all this. He lowered himself into his seat and pulled his hat over his face.

There was the knock of someone's fist on a window very near to him, and then a slap of someone's hand.

'Just go,' whispered Jay quietly, willing Mattie to take him away from Cloncannor.

Jay did not know it in that moment, but some friendships are stronger than the sum of their mistakes. He did not know that the last-minute passenger was Jess. He'd closed his eyes and slouched in the seat to blank out the world. He didn't see her walking towards him or sitting right in front of him. He might never have known she was there until he felt a hand on his hand.

He opened his eyes. 'Jess,' he whispered, 'what are you doing?'

'I'll get straight off at Ennis. I'll never bother you again if you'll just let me talk to you. Only for a minute.'

Jess spoke in breathless spurts, and Jay did not pull his hand away, but looked away from her and out at the green countryside whipping past.

'I understand we can't be friends any more. I'll accept that even though it breaks my heart. But please, Jay, I couldn't bear it if I didn't have a chance to explain.'

'OK, well, now that you're here, you might as well give it a go,' he said, still not looking at her.

'I wanted Bonnie to know what a hero you are. I wanted her to know how much you'd lost. I wanted her to see that someone who's suffered the way you have needs people to be decent to them.'

'I never asked you to protect me from anything,' he mumbled.

'I know. But I wasn't trying to hurt you; I was trying to stand up for you. I just screwed it up, like I screw everything up. If I could be your friend again, I'd do anything, but I'm not asking for that. I know you hate me.'

He looked at her. 'You betrayed me. My father betrayed me. I'm not a hero. I'm a fool.'

Jess stared at him, acknowledging her part in his pain.

He carried on. 'I don't know the difference between what's true and what's not. I can't trust my father. I'm afraid of the lies he has told me.'

'You can trust me,' said Jess. 'I've never lied to you.'

She was right. She'd revealed his secret, but she hadn't lied.

'Where are you going now, what are you going to do?' she asked.

'I'm going to find out the truth, from the only person who can tell it. I'm going to Dublin.'

Jess beamed at him. 'See, I think that's really brave. You have so much courage, Jay.'

'It's not. I don't. I never asked for any of this.'

'Does she know you're coming?'

'No. There wasn't time.'

'Do you want me to text her?'

'That would be great. Thanks.'

So they consulted Jay's ripped email and got the number and Jess told Jay's mother that he was on his way. And she texted back to tell him to meet her at the Daniel O'Connell statue in the middle of the city.

When they got to Ennis, Jay grabbed Jess's hand tight. 'Don't get off. I want you to come. I'd like it if you stayed on. Come with me.'

CHAPTER 22

JESS

'Holy crap, I'm going to be in the absolute worst trouble ever,' I said, but I didn't really care. Jay began to worry that the parents would call Mattie Feeney and then Mattie would be informed that we were two tearaways and we'd be kicked off the bus at Grangekellig and someone would come to bring us back.

'Leave it with me. I might be able to keep them at bay,' I said to Jay, although I wasn't one bit confident.

I thought about it for a while as we stared out and the familiar places became gradually strange. In the end, I decided on Esme.

Ezz, am OK

> Need you to trust me. Keep parents calm.
> Back soon. Tell Patrick I'm with Jay. Something
> we have to do. Can't explain. We'll be OK. I promise.

I was expecting her to go mad but Esme just messaged back with a thumbs-up emoji and two words. *Stay safe.* She can be a pain in the ass, but recently she'd begun to surprise me.

Jay was still staring out of the window but he was talking to me. 'I can't believe I fell for the lies so completely. I can't believe how much I trusted him, you know? I mean, I didn't have a reason not to – because . . . why would your own father lie to you about the most important thing that's ever happened in your whole life? I'd started to fill in the gaps myself, Jess, to colour in the detail. There were nights when I woke up and I swear I could see the shark coming for my mum. I would hear a kind of "whoomp-zip" noise. It kept echoing in my head for ages, like a vibration. You know, the way a massive bell sometimes echoes after it's stopped ringing. Jess, I swear, I was sure these were my memories coming back. I was sure I could hear the shark tearing my mum apart. But now there's this email and a Dublin address, and, guess what, they weren't memories.

They were nightmares planted in my head by a crazy father.' He clenched and unclenched his fists.

'I don't think your father is crazy,' I suggested, but Jay didn't seem to hear me.

'Why did I not see the signs? When I was in the hospital, he never let any of the doctors talk to me for too long. He was always jumping up and saying that I was tired and I needed to stop talking. And when I asked questions, he got secretive and jittery. He didn't even like it when they were in the room. Same with Lonnie. I remember her going on about how I needed to know what happened. I still don't know.'

'You will soon.'

'He smuggled me away from my old home before there was a chance of me finding out what really happened and then cut me off from the rest of the world by not allowing me to have a phone and banning Wi-Fi. Dad let me think my mother was dead, let me stay awake thinking of the terror of her last moments, and let me feel the shame that her death was because of me. But she never died. She's still alive. She survived. What kind of person would do that to their son?'

I had no answer for him. All I could do was listen.

Some of life's journeys stay vivid, every moment, and others are like a heartbeat or a blink, and we only know we must have finished them because of where we end up. That's how it must have been for Jay on Mattie Feeney's minibus to Dublin. He was too preoccupied to be aware of the ordinary beats and rhythms of distance and time.

He kept telling me about the clues he should have been alert to – they swam in front of him, like part of the nightmare coming into view. When he'd borrowed my phone that day to google 'shark bite Dellabelle' or 'Dellabelle shark attack', he'd found nothing about himself. And then he'd tried to find details of his mother's death and her funeral. But there'd been nothing about that either. The lack of documentary evidence and the frailness of his father's explanations now made him realise that he should have known. The look that darkened his dad's face whenever he tried to talk about any of it – that should have been the biggest clue of all.

We got off the bus at the quays and walked over to the Daniel O'Connell statue and heard the squawks of the Dublin gulls.

His mother wasn't there. We waited for fifteen minutes and for every one of those minutes I couldn't think of a single thing to say that would make this better. Another text pinged in. 'Come to the foyer of the Gresham Hotel!' instructed his mother, and Jay let out this big breath he must have been holding in, and we did and there she was in a huge golden coat sipping tea from a china cup.

I wanted to ask her why she hadn't shown up. Why she hadn't been where she said she'd be. But it wasn't up to me to ask the questions.

'Maman, hello, Maman,' said Jay to this flesh-and-blood woman, who waved and smiled from where she sat, the woman who he'd thought had died fighting for him.

She had green eyes just like Jay, but her smile was different, sort of crooked, sort of thin. 'Gosh, look at you. You're totally fine!' she kept repeating, and I kept on wanting to say '*How do you know?*' but this was one of the times I needed to keep my mouth shut.

It was obvious Jay didn't know what to say.

'Have some tea,' said his mother.

'He doesn't drink tea,' I said.

Jay wasn't in the mood for small talk. He needed to get to the point.

'Did you get injured too?' he asked.

'No, not at all, thankfully,' she said.

'How did you escape?' he said.

'Escape?' said his mother, putting her teacup in its saucer and looking puzzled.

CHAPTER 23

JAY

A bigger truth was beginning to occur to Jay and he stopped. He sat down beside her and looked at his mother and felt a moment of fear and hesitation but it was too late to turn back now. 'You never wrestled a shark, did you?'

'A shark? Goodness, no, nothing like that.' She looked at her watch, clicked her fingers and then ordered a glass of champagne.

'There was no shark. I was never attacked by a shark,' he said.

He remembered everything then, as clearly as if he'd always known.

The boat tearing round the corner of Dellabelle Cove, the sound of its engine above him. The frenzied foaming water. The tip of the propeller slicing his side from under his neck down to his knee and then, his mother, seeing what she had done, screaming his name over and over again in the sinister seeping stillness. Jay remembered his blood flowering into the blue of that French sea.

Jay's mother had crashed into him in a motorboat. There had been no other boy. He was the boy. He'd been injured by his own mother who'd driven a boat at top speed into Dellabelle Cove.

'You were never attacked by a shark, Jay,' his mother repeated. She reached out and clutched Jay's shoulder. He pulled away from her like he was being bitten.

'Jay, darling, I've been wanting to ask: why were you in the water at all? You were supposed to be waiting for me on the beach. That's where I told you to be. Your father was so angry with me, but it wasn't my fault really. I didn't see you. It was an accident. I was going too fast to swerve or stop or reverse. It could have happened to anyone.'

Jay's scar felt as if it was on fire. 'You crashed into me!' he said.

'But I didn't see you,' his mother repeated, staring at her glass of champagne.

Jess gasped and looked as if she might make a lunge for Jay's mother, but Jay said, 'No, Jess, leave it,' and then turned to his mother with a grim calmness. 'Why were you going so fast?'

He already knew the answer. It was something he remembered his dad saying about her. Everything had to be a big moment. The clothes she wore, the parties she threw, the attention she pulled towards herself. She made herself the spectacle and this had been a big one. It became clear as she talked, as she tried to explain what had led her to do the awful thing she'd done. She'd bought a boat. Her plan was to come zipping around the sharp corner of the bay and make a spectacular appearance with the engine racing, glistening in the sun, and she was going to moor the boat in the cove beyond the shallows and then she was going to dive into the water and come up on the beach and Jay was going to be thrilled. She'd planned for it to be something he was never going to forget, and when he was grown-up it was going to be one of the stories he told about his mother and how exciting she was.

There had never been a shark. His mother was the shark. She'd nearly killed him.

There was no point in hanging around, hoping she might apologise. He couldn't bear to look at her. She wasn't even sorry. She'd never felt guilt about it, he realised. She'd lured him here to justify herself in some twisted way.

'It's been such a hellish time for me,' she said.

And that was what made Jay grab Jess by the hand and back away and then begin to run, as if they'd just come face-to-face with something more dangerous than either of them could imagine.

It was dark by the time they got back to Cloncannor.

He burst into the cottage like a wave crashing on the beach.

'I will never trust you again! Why did you cover everything up? I dream about a shark attack that never happened! You planted nightmares in my head. Are you proud of yourself?'

'No,' his dad admitted, his face white with his shame, 'no, I'm not.'

'I thought she was a hero. I thought she was an angel looking down on me. You didn't have the courage to tell me the truth.'

'I didn't think it through,' his dad said, leaning on the stove for support, looking defeated.

'No shit!' Jay's rage had gone cold and he was speaking with a new anger. 'I don't even know who you are any more,' Jay whispered, wishing it was not true.

'I'm sorry, buddy. I'm so sorry,' rasped his dad. 'I keep asking myself what the heck I was thinking. It's been driving me crazy – the lying and the pretending.'

'Driving *you* crazy? I'm the one you lied to. You're the one who did the damage.'

'I know.'

'Why did you let me think it was a shark?'

'I didn't want you to know what your mother had done.'

'But I don't understand.'

'Neither do I, Jay. I was blinded. I wanted to erase what had happened. I couldn't bear the truth of it myself, and then I couldn't bear telling you it either. And when you guessed it was a shark who had injured you, I thought it was better that you thought that. And when you started to remember hearing her voice, I knew I was going to have to elaborate in some way, because I was afraid you'd find out what really happened.'

'Great, so you let me believe I had a dead mother? Oh yeah, inspired, Dad, good one. You must have been thrilled with yourself for that particular brainwave.' Jay paused, his heart pounding. 'She only showed up to show off!' he shouted.

'Exactly. It was bad enough that she left when you

were just a baby. I didn't want you to know that she'd also ploughed into you for the sake of making one of her grand entrances, and then that she ran away rather than face what she'd done. I lied because I loved you.'

'It's not good enough, Dad,' said Jay. 'That's a terrible reason for lying to anyone.'

'*Je suis désolé*,' said his dad.

'Stop it,' said Jay.

'We can sort it out, buddy. We have to. We can be friends again.'

'Dad, listen, I'm not a little kid. What you've done can't be wiped away with a tissue or a pat on the back. Do you hear me? This is your fault, and you can't fix it.'

There was a loud and sudden knock at the door, breaking the silence that hovered between them.

It was Sean Flanagan. 'It's Lonnie,' he gasped.

She'd fallen on the beach. Annie had phoned for the ambulance immediately. There'd been no time to waste. Lonnie was already on her way to hospital in Ennis. The baby was coming.

'You really need to get a phone, Dad,' said Jay.

'I know,' said his dad. 'Jay, I can't leave you here on your own. You have to come with me.'

'No, I don't,' said Jay. 'And I won't.'

He could see his dad frozen for a second, and then he watched him grab the keys and rush out the door.

Jay walked in and out of the rooms of the cottage, for how long he didn't know, worrying about Lonnie and the new baby, and wondering whether this was what it was going to be like from now on: him alone in an empty house.

Then Annie Flanagan called over. She was smiling. There was news. The baby was here, and Dad and Lonnie really wanted to see Jay, and hoped he would come. Annie's car was outside, the engine still running. She could have him there in half an hour.

When Jay first saw Stella, the colour fell out of his face and he could not speak. His dad said Jay should sit down because it looked as if he was about to faint. He made Jay sit on the bed. Jay did not stop looking at his sister. Lonnie told his dad to get some water but Jay said he was fine, he just needed some air and he'd be OK if someone opened a window.

And still he couldn't say anything about the

baby, not even when his dad asked him what he thought of her.

'It might be easier to write it down,' suggested Lonnie, who understood more than he'd given her credit for. Writing felt like a good idea, even though at first he didn't know how to begin.

CHAPTER 24

JESS

O n the bus journey home, I'd texted Esme to ask if the coast was clear. She'd texted back and said Mam and Dad had been frantic and raging at first, but that Esme'd used her exceptional diplomatic skills (her words, not mine) to talk them down from the heights of their fury. She told them to relax, explained that I was doing something grown-up and good and important – looking out for Jay on account of him needing someone to be with him for a significant mission in Dublin.

> I've told them they should give you more space now that you're a teenager. We all should. We can't go on treating you like you're a baby.

> About time ☺ ♥

There was always another beach party at the end of August – usually a night or two before school started again. It was was always an evening of mixed feelings – full of finishings and wrappings-up, and goodbyes.

People were usually in subdued moods and by then the sea was normally getting green around the edges, which was a sign that it would soon be winter-grey, and, OK, maybe there'd be one or two more sparkling weekends on the beach and the surf but as soon as September was over, surfing was banned for me and Jay.

Not even Jay was old enough for winter waves or so they said. Patrick and my parents might have loosened up a bit, but they were still in strict agreement about that.

This year, when the party came around and the bonfires were flickering on the beach and the Cloncannor groups were making their ways across the fields and over the dunes, I didn't feel totally dejected. Jay was starting school in my year and Charlie was home. It took me almost twenty-four hours to tell him everything that had happened since he'd been gone.

'Trust me to be away for the most eventful summer of your life, Jess,' he said. It was great to have him back.

*

There's a part of me that loves the threads of cold that start creeping into the air and the way the wind blows the sand around into small gritty clouds, and how people pull on their old jumpers and beanies and cardigans to cosy up in the approaching chill. And I wouldn't tell everyone this, but I secretly love the smell of new books and stationery and the feeling that a fresh start is around the corner – a new season ahead, a winter and then a spring and then a summer, and, beyond that, another winter, far away still but waiting for us, and who knows what we'd be able to do then. One day I'd be a match for the wildest of winters and I didn't know exactly when that would be but I knew for sure it was getting closer, like a wave somewhere far out in the ocean that was on its way.

Jay and I wandered down to the bonfires with Davy. The old gang was there: Nick, Bonnie, Clara, Cian, Jimmy.

'Hey, can I talk to the two of you, please?' said Nick, looking serious.

'What do you want to talk about?' I asked, feeling brave and ready for pretty much anything.

I thought it was going to be another dressing-down. I thought he'd want to rehash my blabbermouth moments in front of Jay and make me feel terrible about myself again.

But he didn't. And it wouldn't have mattered if he had. Turns out Nick wanted to talk about his brilliant skills on the water.

'You won't out-surf me,' he insisted on announcing, and I was like, 'Who cares? In my world surfing's not a competitive sport. Comparisons are pretty much irrelevant. You're welcome to come out with me anytime you like. I'll be too busy finding my own wave to care about whether you're better than me. Because out there it's just me and the wave I'm on.'

'Fair enough,' said Nick and he said he was looking forward to it and he was going to enjoy being on the water with someone as excellent as me instead of wasting frustrating time with the beginners, which is what he'd spent a lot of time doing at 'the academy,' and he said 'the academy' as if it was some big prestigious thing and not just a couple of jeeps and a few chancers.

But for the first time I think there was respect in his voice, and maybe even a small trace of kindness. He said he'd see me in school, and hoped that we could be friends again, and I was like, 'Yeah, sure, but for your information it wasn't me who stopped being your friend. You're the one who went weird on me.' And he nodded and said I was right, and I guess that's as close as anyone will ever come to getting an apology from Nick Carmody.

'Everything OK?' Jay asked a little later when the crowd had thinned and I was in one of the deckchairs staring into the fire, thinking a thousand thoughts but keeping them to myself. I told him everything was fine, and then in a usual fit of clumsiness I spilled a glug of Coke over my pale dress. 'Oh, would you look at that?' I said. 'Typical me. There goes my new dress. Another catastrophe.'

'Jess,' he said with a serious face, 'it's time for you to stop going on about everything in your life being a catastrophe.'

'Why? It feels like that most of the time.'

'It might feel that way, but it's not. Not really. A catastrophe is a tragic thing. Misfortunate. Ruinous. There's nothing about your life that fits that description. You've got two brilliant parents and siblings who love you. Compared to a lot of other people's lives, yours is pretty peachy. Now MY life, that's a different story.'

'Stop,' I said, holding up my hand as if Jay was traffic. 'I'm not going to allow that, either. If you won't let me call my life a catastrophe, then I'm not going to let you call yours one. Our lives are miracles.

I am a miracle and you are a miracle. Everything's a miracle really, when you think about it.'

We looked over at Stella wrapped in her carrier and snuggled up on Patrick's chest, and at Lonnie who was singing with Charlie's band. It was another thing I loved about this time of year. The band was back together.

We let the magic of it sink in. The miracle that the sun comes up every day and that rain falls out of the sky, and the waves of the ocean build from far out at sea and they rise and peak and crash right here on Cloncannor Bay, and that it happens on other coasts, on Dellabelle Cove, and on beaches and strands and inlets and creeks everywhere all over the world. And it's a miracle that we can catch those waves and that we can stand high on top of them and that as long as we keep our balance those waves will always bring us back.

'You're right. Everything's brilliant, Jess. It really is. We need to spend more time being amazed, the way we used to when we were little kids.'

'Good plan. That's what I'm going for from now on. A permanent state of amazement.'

Jay laughed. 'Maybe not permanent. You wouldn't want to make a fool of yourself.'

Jay's dad had bought him a phone. Finally. It was

a massive relief to be able to text him whenever I needed to, which was often. He told me about a friend of his called Louis and we had a Zoom chat, and Louis only speaks French but he sounds great. He's coming over in October for half-term. And a load of other French people are going to visit too. Friends of Patrick and Jay called Pierre, Marie-Bernard and Tom. They've heard Jay's surfing skills are better than ever. They're all coming over to see for themselves.

It was Jay who suggested we should leave the bonfires and the party for a while and go for a walk. I didn't think they would let us, but when we asked our parents they said it was OK.

'Home before dark,' Jay's dad said.

'That means both of you,' Esme shouted after us, as if she was still the boss of me. And we said, 'Yeah, yeah, yeah, OK,' and the two of us walked along both curves of the beach to the other side where the jetty is.

He told me he hoped we'd always be friends. He said how glad he was to have someone like me.

'Why?' I asked.

'Because of your honesty. Because the truth always tumbles out of you no matter what.'

'Oh god, I know. It's a curse.'

'It's not a curse,' he said. 'It's one of the great things about you.'

And our voices seemed to echo off the water even after we'd stopped talking. We took off our shoes and paddled in the shallows and sat on the rocks and nobody came to get us, and we stayed there until way after it got dark and we lay on the sand and listened to the swoosh of the tide and gazed up at the clear black sky.

CHAPTER 25

JAY

A few days after Stella and Lonnie came home, Jay
woke early, and although it was a Saturday and
he had nowhere to be, he was too alert to stay in bed.
He wriggled his sockless feet into his runners, threw
on his dressing gown, headed towards the beach and
sat close to the water, watching a thin hem of foam
fizzing and bubbling in a roll along the sand.

It was a gentle morning, too flat for decent surf,
but as the glimmer on the water stilled in a clouding
sky, he saw someone out there, paddleboarding, a
silhouette against the gun-metal water. The paddler
was far out in the bay but seemed to spot Jay and
began moving towards him, back in the direction of
the beach.

It was his dad, and for a moment Jay remembered
the simple, sunny, happy years and was sad those

times were over. They would have ended sometime no matter what, even if it wasn't for the shark and the scar and the lies and the truth. You can't just hang out with your dad forever in the diamond-scattered waters of a small French town. It was lovely. But for the first time he could see new pathways branching out in front of him, directions he could choose.

He knew he would never see his mother again. Jay would only drive himself crazy if he spent the rest of his life thinking of the years she hadn't shown up and how she had never saved him from anything, especially not a shark. There was no point in envying other people for their mothers. Annie Flanagan was a great mum, and he already knew that Lonnie was going to be great for Stella too. Nick Carmody had a mum who was kind and friendly and who made delicious cakes, which goes to prove that just because you have a wonderful mother doesn't mean you're going to be great yourself. *Take Nick as a perfect example. His mother is class, but Nick is an idiot. Life's a lottery like that.*

In the end, Bonnie told Jay that, as far as she was concerned, he was every bit as brave to have survived the propeller, which if you think about it, is easily as dangerous as a shark, probably more so. The shark hadn't been real, but the scar was and he would have to carry that with him.

Jay didn't talk to his dad for a while. His dad said it was fine; he understood. In some ways the whole story about the shark still kind of broke Jay's heart but sometimes it even made him laugh a bit. Not like a huge laugh. Just a small grown-up kind of chuckle, and only once in a while. He still wished his dad hadn't let him go on believing in a thing that never happened. It would have been fairly handy if a major portion of his identity hadn't been built on a fragile sandcastle of untruths.

Lonnie agreed that Jay had a right to be furious with his father. She told Jay that he didn't have to talk about any of it if he didn't want to, but suggested again that it might be useful to write some of it down.

Hey, Stella, hello. Welcome to the world.

I was angry when I first found out you existed. I'm sorry to admit it. I mean, it's not your fault for existing. And anyway, now I'm glad you do. There was a lot going on at the time. It took me a while to get used to the thought of my dad and your mum being together. I never really knew my mum. It's a long story, and it mightn't even matter by the time you can read this, but I once thought my mother was dead, so I was sort of touchy with anyone else whose mother was alive, including you.

When I heard that you were coming, I worried there would be less love to go around. I didn't think there'd be room for another person. I thought love was like an ordinary thing like cornflakes or orange juice or petrol or paint. I thought it might run out.

But love is not like other things. It's more like the ocean. It's endless and huge and massive waves of it keep on coming even when you're not expecting it.

I thought Lonnie would be hypnotised when you came. (She was. She is.) I thought she hated me. (She didn't. She doesn't.) But, more than this, I thought I was going to lose my dad, that he'd be submerged in his new love for you and totally forget his old love for me. But I've got over those thoughts.

You came earlier than anyone expected. You almost got born on the beach. Everyone was very surprised. Dad and I were in the middle of the biggest argument of our lives. When he heard you were on your way I thought he was going to have a heart attack.

You're absolutely tiny. I sometimes watch you when you're sleeping and look at your ears and

258

your fingernails and your elbows. It's impressive the way you already know how to stretch and yawn and how big your voice is for someone so small.

After your bath you smell brilliant with your baby-powder glow. You don't always smell like that. Your poop is impressive in its own way but disgusting.

Every so often our dad is probably going to do something gigantically stupid and you'll look at him and ask yourself how on earth you're even related to him. But I don't think you'll ever be able to doubt that he loves you.

I know a lot about sharks, and as soon as you can understand words, I'm going to teach you that they're older than trees, how sailors used to call them 'sea dogs', that divers often swim alongside them in total safety, that sharks are colour-blind and that every year millions of sharks are killed by getting tangled up in fishing nets.

I'm not going to hide my scar from anyone any more, especially not from you. And as soon as your eyes can focus, you'll be able to see it, and so you'll never stare or point or think there's anything wrong with having a mark on your body. You'll just know it as a familiar thing. A thing that's part of me.

One day Jessie and I are going to take you surfing.

To be a good surfer you have to be clear-eyed and brave, and you have to fix your sights on a wave and trust yourself and be prepared to be wiped out, to risk it for the thrill. The waves at Cloncannor are sometimes wild and big. They can come at you, huge and frightening. There'll be times when they'll knock you over and you'll have to struggle to get out from under them, spluttering and gasping for breath. Don't be afraid. You'll learn to judge them and get the better of them, and rise on top of them. I already have a feeling you're going to be a natural.

That's it for now, little sibling. I'll sign off with two more promises.

Promise number one: I'm not going to lie to you about anything ever, even when it hurts to tell the truth, which sometimes it will. Promise number two, and this one you can definitely depend on: I'm never going to change your nappy.

Love,
Jay

260

ACKNOWLEDGEMENTS

This book could not have been written without my amazing editor, Rachel Boden. I'm hugely grateful for the care and insight she brought to this story. Thanks also to the brilliant team at Hachette UK and Ireland, including Laura Pritchard, Dominic Kingston, Jennie Roman, Michelle Brackenborough and Siobhan Tierney. Love and thanks to Jo Unwin for her generosity and all-round fabulousness, and to my colleagues and friends at UL, especially Eoin Devereux, Donal Ryan, Joe O'Connor, Eoin Reeves, Sarah MacCurtain, Carrie Griffin, Tina O'Toole and Meg Harper. Thanks also to Melanie Sheridan, Rachel Widdis, Tom Samuels, Kelly Molony, Ashlee De Costa, Louise O'Neill, Marian Keyes and Justine Carbery.

I'm very lucky to be part of a Limerick-based writing group and I'm thankful to all of them, particularly Gráinne O'Brien for being magnificent, and Sheila Killian who patiently surrendered an entire Saturday morning to helping me figure out the thing about the earphones. Thanks to all the members of the SMF online book club who have been a lifeline and a tonic through the strange times and beyond. Special appreciation is due to my darling cousin, Joe O'Dea, for being such a classy host, and for providing me with the best writing retreat any writer could ever need. Here's to Padua, Joe. It matters to me more than I can explain.

Huge love and gratitude to all the Moores, O'Deas and Fitzgeralds, particularly Eoghan, Stef and Gabbie who make me so proud, and to Ger who brings a narrative arc to life that's even better than fiction. Finally, this book is dedicated to the memory of my father-in-law, Hughie Fitzgerald, whose gentle spirit has been one of the blessings of my life.

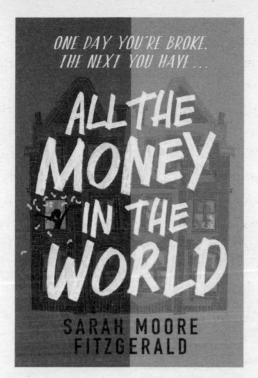

ONE DAY, YOU'RE BROKE.
THE NEXT YOU HAVE...

ALL THE
MONEY
IN THE
WORLD

SARAH MOORE
FITZGERALD

*EVERY DAY, PENNY DREAMS
OF A NEW LIFE ...*

A LIFE FAR AWAY FROM HER FAMILY'S
COLD, DAMP FLAT.

A LIFE FILLED WITH THE KIND OF JOY
HER BULLIES CAN ONLY DREAM OF.

A LIFE WHERE SHE CAN FINALLY SHOW
EVERYONE WHAT SHE'S TRULY CAPABLE OF.

THE LIFE SHE KNOWS SHE CAN *NEVER* AFFORD.

BUT THEN, ONE DAY ...

MORE BRILLIANT BOOKS

BY
SARAH MOORE FITZGERALD